Raquelle.

She was standing on the walkway, in a state of shock.

As he left the SUV and raced toward his ex-wife, Landon had an unnerving sense of foreboding.

I have to stop her, Landon told himself, putting on even more speed as he crossed the walkway in record time.

Before Raquelle could literally plunge herself into the fire, the terrible consequences unthinkable for him, Landon caught up to his ex and grabbed her from behind, stopping her tall and still nicely slender frame in its tracks.

When she looked over her shoulder and glared at him with piercing brown eyes beneath thin brows, a dainty nose, full mouth and dimpled chin on a beautiful diamond-shaped face, as if he were the enemy, he remained firm in telling her, "There's nothing you can do to save him."

EXPLOSION AT THE MARINA

R. BARRI FLOWERS

INTRIGUE

In loving memory of my cherished mother, Marjah Aljean, a devoted lifelong fan of Harlequin romance and romantic suspense novels, who inspired me to excel in my personal and professional lives. To H. Loraine (Sleeping Beauty), the true and dearest love of my life and very best friend, whose support has been unwavering through the many terrific years together; as well as the many loyal fans of my romance, suspense, mystery and thriller fiction published over the years. A special shout-out goes to a wonderful group of talents whom I have long admired: Carol, Charmian, Hedy, Krista, Lisa, Peggy, Olivia and Sharon. And last but not least, a nod to my superb Harlequin editor, Emma Cole, for the wonderful opportunity to lend my literary voice and creative spirit to the Intrigue line, as well as Miranda Indrigo, the wonderful concierge, who serendipitously led me to great success with Harlequin Intrigue.

Harlequin®
INTRIGUE™

ISBN-13: 978-1-335-69053-1

FSC
MIX
Paper | Supporting responsible forestry
FSC® C021394
www.fsc.org

Recycling programs for this product may not exist in your area.

Explosion at the Marina

Copyright © 2026 by R. Barri Flowers

Harlequin Enterprises ULC
22 Adelaide St. West, 41st Floor
Toronto, Ontario M5H 4E3, Canada
www.Harlequin.com

HarperCollins Publishers
Macken House, 39/40 Mayor Street Upper,
Dublin 1, D01 C9W8, Ireland
www.HarperCollins.com

Printed in Lithuania

R. Barri Flowers is an award-winning author of crime, thriller, mystery and romance fiction featuring three-dimensional protagonists, riveting plots, unexpected twists and turns, and heart-pounding climaxes. With an expertise in true crime, serial killers and characterizing dangerous offenders, he is perfectly suited for the Harlequin Intrigue line. Chemistry and conflict between the hero and heroine, attention to detail and incorporating the very latest advances in criminal investigations are the cornerstones of his romantic suspense fiction. Discover more on popular social networks and Wikipedia.

Visit the Author Profile page at Harlequin.com.

CAST OF CHARACTERS

Raquelle Jernigan—An associate theater professor in the town of Joyllis Hills, South Carolina. With her brother nowhere to be found after his pontoon blew up, she must work with her ex-husband to solve the mystery, while they grapple with unresolved emotions from their marriage.

Landon Briscoe—An FBI special agent with the Bureau's Art Crime Team. When his CI goes missing, Landon connects this with the stolen and counterfeit Native American art case he is working on. He enlists his ex-wife to help find her brother during the investigation, while hoping for a second chance at romance between them.

Eddie Jernigan—An art dealer with a target on his back after passing incriminating intel to the FBI in their case against a crime organization. Did being a snitch cost him his life?

Katie Kitagawa—An FBI special agent determined to prove herself in bringing to justice those individuals facing various RICO charges in their investigation.

Ivan Pimentel—A crooked international art dealer who will stop at nothing to cover up his numerous crimes—that includes resorting to kidnapping and murder.

Yusef Abercrombie—The right-hand man of Pimentel, willing to do whatever's necessary to protect both their interests.

Fred Davenport—A skilled bomber hired to do a job and undeterred by any obstacles in his way.

Prologue

Eddie Jernigan drove his white Audi Q4 Sportback e-tron down Yarley Road in South Carolina, trying his best to stay under the speed limit. Problem was he was in a hurry to get to his boat. There, he had collected evidence that the FBI needed to crack a case. His brown eyes peered up at the rearview mirror, then switched to the driver's-side mirror and back. He was sure he was being followed.

Which vehicle was it? Perhaps the dark gray Ford Ranger truck that seemed like it had trailed him for miles?

Or could it have been the white Hyundai Santa Fe SUV that he could swear had matched him when switching lanes, while deliberately keeping a vehicle or two between them, as though playing with him?

Whichever way he sliced it, Eddie was sure that they were onto him and would do whatever it took to stop him at all costs.

At least it could be very costly to him. They wanted him dead.

He drew in a deep breath and refocused on the road ahead as he neared the marina. In that moment, he found himself taking stock of his life. Things had not worked out entirely as he would have wanted in an ideal world.

He'd made some mistakes. And tried to fix them. But was it too late?

Eddie chewed on his lower lip while thinking about his sister, Raquelle. He was a year younger at thirty-three and knew that he'd disappointed her. She had set an example of the right things to do in her life, with their parents no longer around to give them direction and make sure they lived up to their potential.

Raquelle was still dealing with a divorce and couldn't seem to decide who was to blame between her and the ex. Eddie could hardly blame either of them. Not when he'd had trouble maintaining any worthwhile relationship, having recently broken up with his girlfriend, Penelope. Relationships could be hard to maintain. Even with the best of intentions—sometimes the heart was in the right place at the wrong time.

But family was even more important. Maybe it wasn't too late after all to make things right in his life. Especially with Raquelle. He wanted that more than anything. At the very least, he owed her that much.

Not to mention what he owed himself: a chance to put the past behind him once and for all and see what else life could bring that was positive.

Yeah, that's what I'll shoot for, Eddie thought, feeling emboldened as he turned onto Knotter Marina Drive. But first, there was some unfinished business that needed his attention. He glanced at the rearview mirror again, expecting to see one of the vehicles that had trailed him. He saw neither.

Had it only been his imagination? Paranoia had kicked in like a splitting headache.

Breathing a sigh of relief, he ran a hand through his

black hair, styled in a curly mullet, then pulled into the parking lot of the Knotter Marina.

After sighing again, Eddie exited the car, his frame tall and lanky, as he raced across the dock toward the Crest Savannah 250 SLSC pontoon boat he owned that was his pride and joy, in spite of everything else. Glancing over his shoulder, he saw no one who seemed to be paying any particular attention to him.

That's good, he thought with a crooked grin, wanting to believe this wasn't simply the calm before the storm. Maybe he had bought just enough time to get what he needed to protect himself and start to turn things around.

At this point, that was pretty much all he could hope for.

Eddie stepped onto the boat and immediately headed for a midship drawer. He pulled out a cotton duffle bag, unzipped it, and studied the contents inside for a long moment before zipping it back up.

He took out his cell phone and called his sister. No answer. *Pick up*, he pleaded to himself.

Instead, it went to her voicemail.

He left her a stressed message that ended with, "Love you, sis."

After disconnecting, Eddie made another short call, again forced to leave a message, before tucking the phone into the back pocket of his jeans. He grabbed the duffle bag and was just about to head out when he saw a tall, dark-haired man who was walking down the dock. In the direction of his boat.

Tensing, Eddie feared things were about to get ugly— for him. What should he do? Was there a way out of this? Or had he finally bitten off more than he could chew?

He sucked in a deep breath and glanced again at the man who looked familiar and was clearly coming his way, as though on a mission to silence him. Forever.

His heart pounding with dread, Eddie hid from view while wondering if that would possibly be enough to keep him out of harm's way.

Only when the man walked by the boat innocently, never even looking in his direction, did Eddie believe that he had overreacted to the threat.

Or had he?

Could his world still turn upside down?

Would the next close call be the one that finished him off?

He thought about sending Raquelle another text, telling her to disregard the earlier one. But this would likely confuse her even more. He would call her later and try to explain, not sure how she would react while hoping for the best.

Or was he screwed whichever way the pendulum swung? And she would be left to deal with the repercussions.

THE MAN SIZED UP the pontoon and couldn't help but think that it was a boat he wouldn't mind owning himself under other circumstances. But there were no other circumstances. Only here and now. And he had a job to do that left no room for fantasizing. Or second-guessing.

He had trailed the target in a brown Toyota Tundra pickup, trying hard to keep him off guard as Eddie Jernigan drove his Audi erratically, as if he knew that he was being tailed.

And that his number was nearly up.

He walked inconspicuously down the dock, giving a friendly nod to an attractive elderly couple passing by, reminding him of his own grandparents. Though they would undoubtedly disapprove of his chosen lifestyle, what they didn't know wouldn't hurt them. Or him—if he played his cards right.

As if on a leisurely stroll, he deliberately moved past the Crest Savannah 250 SLSC, never even bothering to look at it. This would likely give Jernigan, whom he'd already spotted aboard the boat, a false sense of security. Which was the plan.

It would prove to be the snitch's undoing when the moment of impact came.

Chapter One

"*Hey, sis, I'm at the boat. Hate to have to burden you with this, but, uh...I'm in trouble.*" There was a pause. "*I've done some things and tried to rectify them. Not sure if I can get through this in one piece. Talk to Landon.*" A deep sigh. "*If it doesn't work out, just know that I'm sorry. Love you, sis.*"

The phone went dead.

Raquelle Jernigan's heart skipped a beat. She listened to the cryptic voicemail message from her brother, Eddie, again as she hurriedly walked across the parking lot of Braedon College in Joyllis Hills, South Carolina, where she was an associate theater professor with the fall semester underway.

What have you done, Eddie? Raquelle asked herself worriedly while trying to call him back, only to have it go straight to his voicemail. She knew that he hadn't always walked the straight and narrow in his life's choices. Usually, though, it was fixable and otherwise had solutions that kept him out of jail.

But this time it sounded serious.

Almost a life-and-death issue.

And what did Landon have to do with it?

Raquelle frowned at the thought that her ex-husband,

Landon Briscoe, who was a special agent with the Federal Bureau of Investigation, and her brother were involved in some way. Behind her back apparently.

Now Eddie was frightened enough to leave her a message that almost sounded like a goodbye. The notion unnerved Raquelle, given that he was her only sibling and their parents had passed away.

She reached her blue Infiniti Q50 sedan and got inside, taking the moment she needed to collect her thoughts. She ran thin fingers through thick black hair that fell below her shoulders and was parted in the middle. The color and richness had been inherited from both parents, who, like her and Eddie, were members of the Catawba Nation, a federally recognized Indian tribe in the state of South Carolina. They had also passed on to their children their tall, lean frames and strong jawlines. Not to mention a streak of stubbornness and reluctance toward giving up their independence.

Raquelle started the car and drove off. She trained her brown eyes on the road as she headed to Knotter Marina, on nearby Lake Owenne in Falona County, where Eddie kept his boat.

Her thoughts turned to Landon. They had met at the University of South Carolina in Columbia when she was working on her doctor of musical arts, after getting bachelor's and master's degrees of fine arts in theater from the Department of Theatre and Dance. At the time, he had been pursuing his own graduate degree. They hit it off right away, and things seemed to move full steam ahead from that point.

Upon graduating, they tied the knot, believing that love would resolve any differences they had, no matter how subtle or large. But the hurdles—namely, their differing career objectives and decision to hold off having children—proved to be too much to overcome. After nearly seven years of marriage, they decided to go their separate ways.

Raquelle drew a deep sigh. The divorce was finalized four years ago but almost seemed like yesterday, with the pain from a failed marriage still resonating, even against her best wishes. She had legally ditched his Briscoe and reclaimed her maiden name, Jernigan, in trying to move on as best as possible.

Since then, she and Landon had barely spoken, in spite of ending things on a relatively congenial note. It was as though neither of them wanted to bridge the gap for fear of reopening the old wounds that lingered.

She sometimes wondered if they had made a mistake in ending the marriage instead of going to counseling. Or otherwise putting forth a greater effort to overcome their differences.

No sense in second-guessing now, Raquelle told herself in practical terms. Things were what they were. That included being single at the age of thirty-four. Though she had dated every now and then, no one seemed to interest her the way Landon had once upon a time. How sad was that?

Especially since she had heard through the grapevine that he appeared to have no problem putting himself back out there again. No doubt that women would find him just as irresistible as she once had.

But none of that told her what business he had with her brother. And if that had in any way led to Eddie's present quandary. She tried to get him on the phone again, but he wouldn't—or couldn't—pick up. She thought about taking her brother's advice and calling Landon for an explanation, but she stubbornly clung to preferring to speak to Eddie face-to-face for the scoop.

Pushing back her sense of dread, Raquelle pressed down on the accelerator, while staying within the speed limit as the marina came into view. She turned onto Knotter Marina Drive and pulled into the marina lot, where she found a spot to park.

As she walked across the dock, wearing a new pair of gray wide-leg pants to go with a multicolored split-neck top and flats, Raquelle gazed out at the lake dotted with boats, making for a pretty picture. She barely noticed the tall male who was moving briskly past the marina general store near the end of the dock—other than that he was wearing dark jeans and a blue hooded sweatshirt with the hood over his head and sneakers.

She turned her attention to the various boats of different sizes lining the dock, each undoubtedly carrying an interesting story about the owners and those otherwise occupying the vessels. The same was certainly true for Eddie and his boat. As she came close to it, Raquelle strained her eyes to see if she could see her brother aboard. She thought that she spotted some movement. Or maybe not.

"Eddie," she called out to alert him of her presence when she was a couple of boats away. "Are you there?"

Getting no response, Raquelle got to within one boat of her brother's when suddenly his Crest Savannah 250 SLSC exploded and burst into flames before her very horrified eyes. She screamed in utter shock. For a long moment she was frozen, as if stuck in quicksand. But when this passed, she somehow felt compelled to try and go onto the boat to rescue Eddie, even at risk to her own safety.

Just as she headed in that direction, her pulse skipping a beat, Raquelle felt strong hands holding her back from behind. She looked over her shoulder and into the chiseled heart-shaped face of her ex-husband.

Below black hair in an attractive crew cut, his stone-gray eyes peered at her as he said resignedly, "There's nothing you can do to save him."

In spite of hearing his voice of reason, Raquelle furrowed her brow defiantly, as the enormity of the moment that her brother had been burned alive hit her like a ton of bricks. Beyond that, the fact that Landon happened to be at the scene without her phoning him left her all the more disturbed, in light of Eddie's implication that her ex was instrumental in the circumstances that led to the inferno they were both witnessing like a horror film that was all too real.

And much scarier than Raquelle wished to contemplate.

Two Hours Earlier
Columbia, South Carolina

FBI SPECIAL AGENT LANDON BRISCOE felt the adrenaline rush as he and another agent from the Bureau's Art Crime Team were about to execute a search warrant on Choi's Art Gallery on Main Street in the central business district of downtown Columbia. It was the culmination of a six-month investigation into the theft and illegal trafficking of expensive Asian art by a gallery owner, Nicho-

las Choi, and his associate, art dealer Sheila Hanee. First
reported by law enforcement to the National Stolen Art
File, or NSAF, the FBI's database of stolen art and cultural property, the missing art belonged to the Smithsonian Institute's National Museum of Asian Art.

And will soon be returned to its rightful owner, Landon
told himself, feeling confident. At thirty-six, he stood tall
at six-three—much of his body muscular beneath the FBI
blue vest and professional clothing. He lived for moments
like this, ever since joining the Bureau's Criminal Investigative Division's Transnational Organized Crime unit
three years ago and taking on TOC operations involved
in art-related crimes. The work had him moving between
field offices in Charlotte, North Carolina; Las Vegas, Ne-
vada; and his current location, the FBI Columbia field
office based in Lexington County, in Lexington, South
Carolina. Prior to that, he'd spent more than six years
dividing his time between the Bureau's Environmental
Crime and White-Collar Crime programs.

Landon had attended the University of South Carolina, where he majored in criminology and criminal justice at the College of Arts and Sciences and came away
with a BA, MA and PhD. Not to mention a wife—until
she wasn't one a few years later. Just the opposite of his
own mother, who had recently become a newlywed after
being on her own for years, ever since his father's unexpected death from a cardiac arrest.

Landon returned to the moment at hand as he regarded
Special Agent Katie Kitagawa. Katie was nearly thirty
and slim, with a brunette flipped-out bob and wore round
glasses over hazel eyes. "You ready to do this, Kita?" he

asked, using the nickname she had been given by others in the Bureau as a short to Kitagawa and play on Katie, which she had eventually warmed up to. He already had the answer to the question, knowing full well that she was always prepared to slap the cuffs on any deserving suspect once they had the goods to work with.

"Absolutely." Katie flashed her teeth. "Let's put Choi and Hanee out of business before they can sell any more stolen paintings!"

"All right." Landon put a hand on his Springfield Armory 1911 Tactical Response Pistol with an Agency Optic System, or 1911 TRP AOS .45 ACP caliber handgun tucked into the tan leather tactical holster at his side. "Go," he said, and gave a nod to personnel from the South Carolina Law Enforcement Division, who were assisting in the operation.

Within minutes, they had served the search warrant to a fortysomething, well-dressed female employee with brunette hair in a shag style, who was fully cooperative. Beyond the impressive showroom with its art pieces, Landon discovered what they were looking for in a back room—on display on the walls, as if only for a select audience of buyers.

Nicholas Choi and Sheila Hanee, who had been tracked by other agents while riding together in a white Lincoln Corsair SUV, were stopped and taken into custody without incident.

"Another case for prosecutors to have at it," Katie said satisfyingly as Landon walked to her cypress-gray Chevrolet Tahoe in the parking lot.

"With some major help from us," he pointed out, knowing that their input was imperative for any successful conviction.

She nodded in agreement. "Always."

"Catch you later," Landon said, which was code for at any time—day or night—as their investigations both crisscrossed and went in separate directions, depending on the caseload and, at times, involvement with other law enforcement agencies in cases that overlapped.

He watched briefly as she climbed into her SUV before he moved toward his own dark ash metallic Chevy Tahoe.

It wasn't till he was inside that Landon thought to check his cell-phone messages, having put that on hold while the mission was underway. He lifted the phone from the side pocket of his dark blue trousers and saw that there was exactly one message.

From Eddie Jernigan. His ex-brother-in-law. And current confidential human source.

Landon had recruited him as part of an ongoing investigation into a Native American art theft, forgery, and money-laundering ring. Using his on-again, off-again occupation as an art dealer provided the perfect cover for Eddie to gather information from those operating illegally in the world of art and relay it back to him using a burner phone.

Investigative statement analysis, along with data from the NSAF had indicated to Landon that the info passed along was credible. The fact that Eddie had been implicated himself in the handling (or mishandling) of forged art but given an out with his cooperation gave him more than enough incentive to work with the Art Crime Team.

In addition to putting organized art thieves out of business and into prison, federal law violations of the Native American Graves Protection and Repatriation Act required the repatriation of stolen art or cultural items. At the same time, Landon was promoting continual discourse between those mostly affected, such as American Indian tribes, art museums, and galleries.

Landon had chosen not to divulge to his ex, Raquelle, that Eddie was working for him as a confidential informant, or CI. Not only would it have defeated the purpose of the secretive nature of Eddie being undercover, but the knowledge could have potentially placed her in danger. Even with the somewhat strained—or more like nonexistent—relations between him and his former wife, Landon would never have wanted her to be put in any peril. Eddie made it clear that they were on the same wavelength in keeping Raquelle out of it.

So what does Eddie have for me? Landon asked himself as he listened to the message.

Eddie's voice cracked as he said, "*Landon, I think they've figured out that I'm talking to you... Now they want me dead. You have to help me, man. I'm on my boat. I should've passed on being a snitch.*" He sucked in an erratic breath. "*I need a way out of this—before I'm silenced forever...*" Another uneven sigh. "*If something happens to me, fill Raquelle in on what's been going on... She deserves that much, don't you think?*"

The voicemail ended.

Landon was left with more questions than answers. He called Eddie's number but only got his recorded message of being unable to respond.

That's not good, Landon thought, wondering if there was a sinister reason why he wouldn't—or couldn't—pick up. Eddie had been walking a tightrope, being persuasive to organized offenders he was dealing with and being straight as Landon's CI in dispensing relevant information to the investigation. If they really had made him, he would definitely need to be pulled out, and not just for his sake. For Raquelle's too, as his sister and the person Eddie was probably closest to.

Starting the SUV, Landon headed for Knotter Marina, a short distance away. He made another attempt to reach Eddie but got the same nonresponse. *Hopefully he was able to stave off any threats to his life till help arrived*, Landon thought, trying not to allow himself to assume the worst-case scenario.

His mind wandered off to his ex-wife. From the moment he first laid eyes on Raquelle Jernigan as she walked across the campus of the University of South Carolina, he fell in love with the beauty. She was the complete package physically. And when he struck up the nerve to have a conversation with her, he was even more smitten and impressed with her personality and intellect.

Asking Raquelle to marry him had probably been the best decision Landon ever made. She was the woman he'd dreamed about in so many ways but never thought he would land as a wife, lover, and best friend. Unfortunately, things took a left turn during their six-plus years together, as both seemed to want more than the other could give to be happy. Neither seemed ready to commit to having a family over pursuing their professional goals. That major stumbling block, along with magnifying the little things into something bigger than they were, was more than either could handle. Rather than continue to question each other's choices and commitment to the marriage, which seemed to be nearing the point of no return, they chose to take the easy way out and call it quits.

Looking back, now Landon wondered if they had acted hastily in ruining a good thing. At least that was how he saw their relationship. Those memories he wouldn't trade for anything. Maybe Raquelle saw it differently and had no regrets about ending their marriage.

Since the divorce, neither had gone out of their way to keep in touch for the most part, only bumping into each other on occasion when he was back in the area. He had wanted to reach out to Raquelle from time to time but didn't want to push the envelope if this made her uncomfortable.

Was that a mistake?

Landon had asked Eddie recently if his sister was seeing anyone and the answer was no, but he admitted that Raquelle was pretty private about her social life. So maybe there was hope yet for them.

Or is that a stretch after four years apart? Landon asked himself as he gazed through the windshield at the street ahead. While his own dating life since the divorce had been unfulfilling at best and downright disastrous at worst, he had reconciled himself to the reality that life went on, like it or not. *I can't change the past or make Raquelle feel about me the way she once did*, he thought squarely. He was left with no choice but to play the hand both had been dealt, for better or worse.

Unfortunately, the same was true for Eddie.

For his sake, Landon hoped there might still be light at the end of the tunnel that they both could benefit from.

When he pulled into the marina parking lot, Landon

could see that a boat was on fire. His first thought was that it had to be anyone's boat but Eddie's.

But that belief—or fantasy—went out the window when Landon spotted what looked to be Raquelle. She was standing on the walkway, appearing as though she was in a state of shock.

Even as he left the SUV and raced toward his ex-wife, Landon had an unnerving sense of foreboding that she might feel duty bound to pull her brother from the flames engulfing his Crest Savannah 250 SLSC pontoon.

I have to stop her, Landon told himself, putting on even more speed as he crossed the walkway in record time.

Before Raquelle could literally plunge herself into the fire, the terrible consequences unthinkable for him, Landon caught up to his ex and grabbed her from behind, stopping her tall and still nicely slender frame in its tracks.

When she looked over her shoulder and glared at him with piercing brown eyes beneath thin brows, a dainty nose, full mouth, and dimpled chin on a beautiful diamond-shaped face, as if he were the enemy, he remained firm in telling her, "There's nothing you can do to save him."

Landon wasn't sure if she heard him correctly. Or had deliberately chosen to tune him out. He could only consider that Eddie must have called her as well and possibly mentioned him in the conversation, causing Raquelle to react negatively to their association behind her back.

Gazing at the boat on fire as others began to emerge to see the awful display, Landon could only imagine what must have been going on inside Raquelle's head that was surrounded by long and loose, thick raven hair. He knew that no one could come out of that inferno alive, which was obviously hard for her to accept.

And it would be left for him to deal with the fallout, assuming that Eddie had been unable to escape the horrendous fate that was set in motion through their mutual cooperation.

Chapter Two

Raquelle was on pins and needles as she waited for word on whether or not her brother had succumbed to the flames that ripped through his pontoon like a firestorm. Surely Eddie couldn't still be alive on the boat. And if he was, his injuries would be so severe that she wasn't so sure he would want to keep living, in spite of their appreciation for the gift of life, no matter its unpredictable journey.

As firefighters went to work to put out the flames—after other nearby boats had been evacuated—and people had gathered to gawk as though visiting a tourist attraction, Raquelle turned toward her ex-husband. She was still coming to grips with him being there at the scene—albeit too late to prevent what might have happened to Eddie. Had he called Landon to ask for help? What were the two involved with that had them in close contact?

Raquelle knew that they both got along fairly well during her marriage to Landon. But once it was over, Landon seemed to make a concerted effort to distance himself from both her and Eddie. Her brother seemed to think that this was for the best, as she had. So what changed?

She regarded Landon. Though his chiseled features were hardened, she had to admit that he had changed little since they first met. If anything, he was even more handsome, if possible, than the man she fell in love with years ago. And every bit as fit, judging by the contours of his firm frame beneath the clothing and FBI vest. But he had matured over time, which made him even more appealing to the eye.

Now, though, was not the time to reminisce. Or look beyond the unsettling moment at hand.

Raquelle regarded her ex hotly and asked suspiciously, "What happened here...?"

Landon paused, then responded evasively, "Hard to say at this point. It could be an accident or something else... Why don't we wait and see what the fire marshal says—"

She could tell that he was dodging the issue and wouldn't let him off the hook, considering what had happened. "Eddie told me to talk to you—after leaving me a voicemail, telling me he was in trouble... He seemed to fear for his life—"

Landon ran a hand across his mouth musingly before meeting her gaze. "He had a reason for that... We can discuss it later. For now, I'd rather focus on your brother's current plight and go from there."

Or, in other words, wait to confirm that Eddie is dead before elaborating on the details, Raquelle told herself, reading between the lines. She wasn't really in a position to argue the point, aware of just how obstinate her ex-husband could be at times. Even when acting as an FBI special agent. But she needed to know what was going on that brought him and Eddie together, apparently putting her brother in harm's way.

"All right," she acquiesced.

Landon nodded and went into contemplative mode,

which told Raquelle he was clearly troubled about their being reunited under such scary circumstances. So was she. More than once, she had considered taking the first step in reopening the lines of communication. At the very least, she wanted to come to some better understanding about why things fell apart between them. But as always, it never seemed like the right time. And for his part, as he made no serious effort in this regard, it seemed pointless.

Raquelle's reverie was broken when they were approached by the South Carolina State Fire Marshal Joseph Lieberstein. He was in his fifties and thickset, with graying hair in a short comb-over style and bushy brows. Looking grim, he took a breath as he gazed at her and asked knowingly, "Your brother owned the boat?"

"Yes," Raquelle told him, nerves rattled. "Eddie Jernigan."

Lieberstein nodded and said with a catch to his tone, "The boat was totally destroyed by the fire." A pause. "We didn't find any human remains on the boat," he said flatly.

Raising a brow in disbelief, Raquelle asked him hopefully, "Are you sure?"

"I'm sure," the fire marshal responded. "If anyone was on board beforehand, they were able to escape before the explosion."

Thank goodness for that, she thought, breathing a huge sigh of relief that her brother might still be alive.

Landon stepped toward him and, after flashing his credentials while identifying himself, asked the fire marshal deliberately, "Do you have any idea how the fire started?"

Lieberstein pinched his long nose. "Still in the early stages of the investigation, but it appears as though an explosive device went off on the boat. Whether this was meant more to destroy whatever was on it or targeting the owner in specific, remains to be seen. We've called in the Falona County Sheriff's Office Bomb Squad."

"Okay." Landon frowned. "Someone was definitely sending a message of sorts," he contended. "The sooner we can get to the bottom of it, the better for everyone."

"I couldn't agree more," Lieberstein said and then eyed Raquelle. "Hope you can locate your brother alive and well."

"Me too," she told him. The notion of a bomb detonating on Eddie's boat—likely intended to go off with him on it—frazzled Raquelle's emotions. She watched the fire marshal walk away, then she turned to Landon. "I saw a man wearing a hoodie, running away from the boats," she recalled. "Could he have been responsible for the explosion—believing that Eddie was on his boat...?"

"It's possible," Landon conceded. He regarded her thoughtfully. "Could it have been Eddie that you saw leaving the scene of the crime?"

"Eddie?" Raquelle batted her lashes. "No! I'm sure I would recognize my own brother—thank you." She understood that he was asking the question in more of an official capacity than as a former brother-in-law. Or ex-spouse. Still, the mere suggestion that Eddie might have blown up his own cherished boat was way off base.

"Had to ask." Landon's voice softened guiltily. "We'll see what investigators and surveillance cameras come up with. In the meantime, if Eddie is still alive, we need to find him."

"You're right—we do." Raquelle was glad that he wasn't shutting her out. At least in this instance, in which she had to know that her brother was okay. She still needed Landon to be upfront with her on whatever information he had on this situation.

"We can start off by seeing if Eddie's at his apartment." Landon brushed against her shoulder, causing an immediate ripple effect throughout Raquelle's body. "I'll follow you there. And keep trying to see if you can reach him by phone. Or if he tries to contact you in any way, let me know."

"I will," she promised and headed with him to the parking area while managing to keep her emotions in check for now.

LANDON WAITED FOR her to get inside her vehicle. He started to say something but held up, not believing it was the time to say more about Eddie and his possible fate. "See you in a bit," he said instead and stood mute till she drove off.

Heading to his own SUV, Landon took out his cell phone and called Katie Kitagawa to share the disquieting news about Eddie.

She picked up with a teasing, "Hey. Miss me already, Briscoe?"

Normally, he might have found an appropriately amusing comeback, knowing that she was happily dating Tony Razo, the US marshal for the District of South Carolina. Instead, Landon got right to the point as he said tersely, "My CI's boat just exploded."

"Seriously?" Katie asked shockingly.

"Yeah. Went up in flames at the Knotter Marina. The fire marshal thinks it was a bomb."

"Wow." She muttered an expletive. "Was anyone on it?"

"No, thankfully. It was unoccupied." Landon sighed. "Unfortunately, I haven't been able to reach Eddie."

Katie paused. "You think he's dead?"

"Don't know." It was an honest answer but a shaky one at best. Landon reached his Tahoe. "I'm heading over to his place now."

"Have you spoken to your ex about this?" she asked tentatively.

"Briefly," he answered musingly, having been upfront with her and the Bureau about his relationship with Eddie. It—or he—was seen as an asset rather than a liability in gaining important intel on the underbelly of the art world. "Raquelle was at the marina when I got there. Eddie left her a voicemail indicating something was up—without elaborating. Needless to say, she's not taking this very well. Neither am I."

"Not too surprising," Katie told him. "But you don't know what you don't know as to Jernigan's status…"

"True." Landon got inside the SUV. He wouldn't get too far ahead of himself, resolving to keep an open mind, within reason.

After they disconnected, Landon contacted the Bureau's Weapons of Mass Destruction Directorate's Investigations and Operations Section to report a possible WMD incident, assuming Eddie's boat was, in fact, bombed. The FBI would, as always, coordinate its efforts with the Falona County Sheriff's Office Bomb Squad and certified explosives specialists from the Bureau of Alcohol, Tobacco, Firearms, and Explosives in getting answers.

For Landon's part, with Eddie as his CI in a major federal investigation, and possibly missing in action, there was an even greater sense of urgency here to solve the case and locate his ex-brother-in-law. And then there was Raquelle. The ordeal of seeing her brother's boat burst into flames before her very eyes had to weigh heavily on her. The only way of getting that vision out of her head would be to find Eddie still alive and in good health. And able to stay that way.

Both could be a high bar to clear, from Landon's point of view. He had a sense that the explosion was much more than making a statement. Or sending a message. Though it wasn't totally implausible that Eddie could have blown his own boat to smithereens, perhaps to throw pursuers off the trail, Landon seriously doubted he would take such extreme measures. He knew that Eddie treasured his boat like one might a newborn baby. As such, it was inconceivable that he would want to destroy it.

Moreover, Eddie didn't have it in him to do something that put other boats and their occupants at risk just to save his own skin.

That left Landon certain that the explosion was likely the work of the art-crime syndicate that Eddie was trying to help them to bring down.

How had Eddie managed to avoid a date with death? Or had he?

Landon considered the man who Raquelle spotted fleeing the scene. He agreed with her that had it been Eddie, she would have recognized him. Unless she only saw the man wearing a hoodie with a passing glance and, as such, never truly homed in on him with clarity.

I'll give Raquelle the benefit of the doubt that it wasn't Eddie she saw, he told himself as he followed her car to Eddie's residence in the nearby town of Gadwall Heights. Landon feared that Eddie, if alive, would not have gone there if he believed they were onto him and figured out that he wasn't on the boat.

But what if Eddie never got the opportunity to escape?

Landon was bothered by the fact that neither he nor Raquelle had heard from her brother. If Eddie felt his back was up against the wall, wouldn't he reach out for help to either the FBI or the person he cared most about (apart from himself) in the world?

I can't put myself inside the man's head, Landon thought smartly, even if as his CI and former brother-in-law he had gotten a fair read on Eddie. Or had he?

After arriving at the Bechum Apartments complex on Klatton Road, which was close to a forested area, Landon got out of the SUV and walked up to Raquelle, who was waiting for him.

"I have a key," she said, holding it up for his eyes. "Eddie wanted me to hang on to his spare one, in case I ever needed to drop by for any reason and he wasn't around."

"Nice of him," Landon said, wishing he had thought of extending the same offer to her to stay at his house when he moved back to the greater Columbia region. Would she have accepted? "Do you see his car anywhere?" He scanned the parking lot, looking for Eddie's white Audi Q4 Sportback e-tron.

"No—it's not here," Raquelle told him, a note of regret in her tone.

"Maybe he left the car elsewhere deliberately and walked the rest of the way." Landon wasn't sure he bought that but wanted to hold out hope that Eddie was holed up inside. "Let's check it out."

"All right."

"I lead, you follow," he warned her, in case they ran into trouble.

Raquelle didn't argue the point, but she was clearly anxious to appease her worry regarding her brother's whereabouts.

Landon walked up to the door of the third-floor unit. Before he could ask Raquelle for the key, he could see that the door was slightly ajar. Instinctively, he pulled out his firearm and told her, "Wait here."

Though seemingly irritated at the order, she complied. He kicked the door open and went inside to check it out. His feet were firmly planted on the hardwood floor as Landon looked for any signs of movement.

The place had been ransacked. While he had never known Eddie to be a neat freak, it was obvious to Landon that someone had done a number on the apartment, its contemporary furnishings turned upside down, inside out. Clearly, someone was looking for something, apart from Eddie himself.

When Landon finished checking out the two-bedroom apartment, he found Raquelle standing in the doorway, looking shell-shocked as she took in the mess before her. "Eddie's not here," he told her, as if this would somehow appease her, given what she was looking at. "So don't come any further, as this has to be considered a crime scene now—"

Raquelle peered at him but did move an inch. "Who did this, Landon?" she demanded. "I need to know what's going on with my brother, as you obviously do." Her tone lowered an octave. "Please…"

Between the mesmerizing glint in her brown eyes, a pout on those full lips, and the stark realization that this was not something he could keep from Raquelle any longer, he was feeling contrite that her brother's life might well be hanging in the balance.

Landon met her at the door. "I need to call this in," he said. He wanted to get the investigation rolling in what was clearly a felony breaking and entering, based on the damage, and overlapped between local and federal jurisdiction, under the circumstances. "Then we can talk in your car."

Chapter Three

Raquelle regarded Landon, ill at ease, as she sat behind the wheel of her Infiniti Q50 and waited to hear what he had to say about her brother's worrying situation.

After taking a breath, Landon met her eyes squarely and said in a measured tone of voice, "Eddie's been working undercover for the FBI—actually me—as a confidential human source, or confidential informant…"

Her lashes fluttered with surprise. "He what?"

"He's my CI," Landon reiterated briefly. "Eddie's been providing crucial information on an art-theft-and-counterfeit-art ring I'm investigating."

Raquelle understood this. After all, she'd been married to the man and knew some of the lingo and requirements of the job. But that didn't make hearing that he had involved Eddie in something obviously dangerous any easier to digest. "Why would he work for you—at risk to his own safety?" Though she knew that her brother dabbled in the art world, selling some Native American art he was able to acquire from time to time, that was still a stretch from becoming her ex's CI. She needed to hear more.

As though reading her mind and anxieties, Landon leaned forward and said flatly, "Eddie was under investigation for selling forged art. Rather than go after him—something that I didn't have the power to simply sweep under the rug, even if I'd wanted to—I asked Eddie instead to become my CI. Knowing that he had the ins to some bad guys involved in the murky world of art crimes, it was a win-win. He wouldn't end up being charged and, most likely, convicted and forced to spend time behind bars—and the Art Crime Team, which I've spent the last three years working for with the Bureau, would use what Eddie provided to build our case and put those under investigation away for a long stretch."

Raquelle wrinkled her nose at him and asked irrationally, "Couldn't you have picked someone else to do your dirty work other than my own brother?"

"It wasn't a question of choice per se but opportunity and timing." Landon moved uncomfortably in the passenger seat. "Eddie knew the risks—and also the rewards of staying out of jail. He was his own man, and he opted to take this path."

Raquelle didn't doubt for one minute that her brother knew what he was doing. Nor did she believe that Landon—or anyone else—could compel Eddie to act against his own best interests. But had those turned to worst interests? *What have you gotten yourself into, Eddie?* she asked, given the dire conditions he faced.

She eyed her ex-husband and, pursing her lips, demanded, "Why didn't you tell me what was going on? As your ex-wife, I deserved to know that Eddie was working undercover for you and what it entailed…"

"That's not the way this works, Raquelle," Landon told her, as if she needed to be reminded. He did so anyway. "As an FBI special agent, I'm bound to separate professional from personal parts of my life. Telling you would have potentially blown Eddie's cover and jeopardized the case. Not to mention possibly putting you in harm's way. I couldn't let that happen. And Eddie felt exactly the same way." Landon jutted his chin. "Apart from that, you and I haven't really been on speaking terms—or so it seemed—for the last few years. Not exactly a way I wanted to break the ice...by talking about your brother violating the law and a remedy for that."

Raquelle conceded that neither he nor Eddie had been obligated to confide in her about the investigation. Yes, she and her ex hadn't communicated very much since the divorce—no matter the rationale or lack thereof. She hated to think that Eddie had chosen to skirt the law instead of coming to her for help, if he had money problems. She was hardly a rich divorcée—far from it—even with a few investments in the stock market that she'd made when she was still married to Landon. But she had socked away some money that she would gladly have given her brother, if it meant staying out of trouble. And forced to be a confidential human source for the FBI as a result. Now she didn't even know if he was alive or dead.

"Okay, I get it," Raquelle said, meeting Landon's firm gaze. "You both did what you needed to do." She paused thoughtfully. "Why was Eddie's place trashed? What were they looking for...?"

Landon scratched his chin, ruminating, before he responded, "My guess is that they were looking for any damning evidence that could be used against them as we pursue our case—assuming there wasn't anything else going on in Eddie's life that he kept to himself. The ransacking could have come before, during, or after the boat explosion at the marina."

Sucking in a calming breath, she asked fearfully, "If Eddie wasn't on the boat and isn't at his apartment...is he on the run or what?"

Landon did not pull any punches when he replied unwaveringly, "It may well be *or what*. I don't want to lead you astray by suggesting that Eddie is in hiding. Some very bad people apparently want him dead—and he's not answering his cell phone. Or otherwise trying to contact one of us for help. That tells me he may not have made it out of this alive." Landon put his hand atop hers. "On the other hand, there's been no body found or other verification that he's stopped breathing. You know your brother better than I do, Raquelle, so you should go with your own instincts on this—until proven otherwise..."

She stilled her nerves. *I have to believe Eddie's still alive, in spite of the current trajectory*, she told herself. To give up hope was not in her DNA. Even against the odds that seemed to be in play. "Okay."

He took his hand off hers and said, "I have to go. If Eddie does get in touch with you, let me know immediately."

"I will," she promised. Then added, "Back at you."

Landon nodded. "All right."

Raquelle watched him get out of the vehicle while feeling there was so much more to be said regarding where things stood between them. Would the opportunity ever present itself to go there without the specter of Eddie's disappearance hanging over them like a shroud? Clouding any possible chance of a reconciliation of sorts?

She started up her car and headed home.

RAQUELLE DROVE UP to her custom contemporary house on Velick Road in Dryer Woods, not far from the college or Knotter Marina. It was two stories with four bedrooms and sat on a forested two-acre lot that had loblolly pine and southern red oak trees, and a trail that meandered through them. She had hoped to find Eddie's Audi Q4 Sportback e-tron on the concrete driveway, thinking he might have come there for safe refuge. But it wasn't there. Her eyes scanned the property for any sign of him. Again, she came up empty. Maybe he thought it best to keep his distance while trying to figure things out. Or was that more wishful thinking on her part?

The realistic thought that her brother was dead left Raquelle feeling nauseous but unconvinced. Wouldn't she be able to sense it somehow if this were the case? Could she really trust her senses in the face of witnessing his boat exploding and seeing firsthand that his apartment had been ransacked? Surely, these were bad signs that she couldn't dismiss out of hand. Any more than the fact that Eddie had chosen to involve himself in art theft as if he had no choice in the matter, much to her chagrin.

Still, she needed to just wait and see how things played out, no matter the uncomfortable optics.

Raquelle left the car and walked onto a covered porch. Unlocking the front door, she went inside and stood on Brazilian cherry hardwood flooring. She took a moment to admire the downstairs layout that included coffered ceilings, a spacious great room, separate dining room, gourmet kitchen with a two-level island and stainless-steel appliances, and lots of picture windows with drapery. The furnishings were a mixture of traditional and

Native American. A security system was in place to safe-guard the property, inside and out.

Raquelle glanced at the circular stairs leading to the second floor. There were four bedrooms up there, two en suites, a recreation room, and it was all similarly furnished in an attractive style. This was supposed to be their dream home two years after she and Landon tied the knot. Instead, she wound up living there alone once the divorce was finalized after he'd insisted that she keep the house rather than put it up for sale and split the proceeds.

Now Raquelle wondered how different things might have been had they stayed together. Could they have already begun the process of filling the home with children for them to dote over and spoil rotten? Or would they have continued to be at odds over the timing? How would a family have played into their professional and social lives?

Raquelle stepped further inside the great room to a corner where there was a black handcrafted upright piano and padded bench. She sat on it. Having learned to play at an early age, Raquelle had carried this into adulthood, mainly as a stress reducer. Admittedly, she had enjoyed playing more when she could do so for Landon. Or with him, when he played his guitar. Had the thrill waned with him too over the years?

She played a few notes thoughtfully before heading for the kitchen to take out some leftovers for dinner.

LANDON HAD WAITED patiently for more than two hours at the marina as boats had been temporarily evacuated by authorities while explosives-detection canines searched for other possible bomb threats. Bomb technicians from several jurisdictions pored over the charred boat belonging to Eddie. At least it had before being totally ruined and he went missing. On that note, it would only go one of two ways. Either he had been killed and maybe buried in an unmarked grave or out in the lake or Raquelle's brother had fled for his life and was now lying low, panicked, trying to figure out where to go from here.

With the possibility that Eddie had jumped—or been thrown—into the water, before or after the explosion, the South Carolina Department of Natural Resources Division of Law Enforcement had dispatched a dive team to search Lake Owenne for his body. Landon feared what they might find, given the boat's destruction and no sign of Eddie.

No matter how bad things seem, I'd hate for Raquelle to get her hopes up, Landon told himself, even while feeling the same way. Only for her to be let down in a big way if this went south as far as Eddie's existence. For his part, Landon needed him to be alive. Both because of the knowledge that Eddie possessed pertaining to the investigation and, maybe more importantly, he didn't want his former brother-in-law's misfortunes to taint whatever chance Landon had for making things right again with Raquelle.

Or was that an impossible task at this point?

His musings were disrupted when ATF Explosives Enforcement Officer Chelsea Furillo walked up to him. Thirtysomething and slender in her uniform with blond hair pulled back into a topknot and green eyes, she said evenly, "Agent Briscoe, I have info on the boat explosion..."

"Okay. What do you have for me?" He prodded her

along, having already briefed her on the specifics of the art-theft investigation.

"It was caused by an IED."

Landon lifted a brow in considering the acronym, which was short for *improvised explosive device*. "Planted inside the boat?" he asked, as opposed to outside or beneath it.

"Yes," Chelsea confirmed. "We believe that someone snuck on board and placed the IED beneath the engine. The bomb was almost certainly triggered remotely, though likely within reasonably close proximity to the boat."

Landon thought about the man in a hoodie that Raquelle saw close to the scene. "I'm guessing that it was timed to go off with the owner, Eddie Jernigan, on board."

"Makes sense," she said, "unless the bomber intended to blow up certain contents on the boat."

"Could be the unsub was looking to achieve both objectives," Landon argued contemplatively. "If so, the bomber may have only succeeded halfway—with Jernigan's current whereabouts unknown."

Chelsea rubbed her nose. "If he's still out there somewhere, maybe you can get to him before the perp can finish the job."

Landon responded, in thinking about Raquelle, "That would be preferable."

"In the meantime, we'll see what else, if anything, we can dig up as clues about the unsub," she told him. "Though it won't be easy, given that the IED was powerful enough to ignite the gas—all but destroying critical evidence."

He nodded. "Give it your best shot."

"Will do." She walked away.

Landon understood that they would need to rely on a combination of forensic evidence, surveillance videos, witnesses, and any other means to solve this and bring the culprit to justice.

Not to mention track down Eddie. Even though there was the real possibility that he was no longer in a position to cooperate in the case.

Landon watched as one of the DNR divers emerged from the water. Officer Julian Uchida, thirtysomething, tall and muscular, was in full gear as he approached.

"Find anything?" Landon asked hesitantly, not sure what to expect.

Julian shook his head. "Just some debris. No sign of a body submerged in the water."

That's good, he thought. Or at least it kept hope alive, considering the alternative. "Eddie must have gotten out of the boat in time—and in one piece," he surmised.

"We'll search a while longer, to be sure," Julian told him.

"Okay." Landon watched as he headed back to the lake to join the other diver still underwater. Until proven otherwise, Landon had to believe that his CI was still on land—if not buried six feet under somewhere.

AFTER WORK, LANDON HEADED HOME. He had a mind to stop by unannounced at what used to be his house but thought better of the impulse. Raquelle had enough on her plate right now than to be forced to rehash reminiscences with the man who divorced her. Or was it more the other way around?

Whatever the case, he wanted to try and work his way

back into her life in a way that they both felt comfortable with. She needed time to come to terms with Eddie's disappearance, one way or the other. *So do I*, Landon thought, gazing ahead at the traffic. To say nothing of her learning that he had put himself in the unenviable position of being a CI by his own poor choices.

There would be time to get beyond the disappointments and regrets, whichever way the pendulum swung regarding someone who was once his brother-in-law.

And his ex-wife.

Landon drove into the parking garage of his condominium on Hampton Street in downtown Columbia. He parked alongside his off-duty personal vehicle, an autumn-green metallic Subaru Outback.

After taking the elevator up, Landon went inside the two-bedroom, two-and-a-half-bath condo that he had leased six months ago. It had an open concept with maple hardwood floors, high ceilings, and vinyl windows. There was a spacious living room and dining room, with barnwood furniture and a chef's kitchen with quartz countertops. Not that he did much cooking, having no one to feed but himself these days. Maybe that could change.

He went to the kitchen and grabbed a bottle of beer from the French-door refrigerator and opened it, taking a swig. Moving back inside the living room, he gazed at the wood acoustic guitar that was leaning against a rustic microfiber accent chair. It was the same guitar he owned when he first met Raquelle. She used to love watching him play some country, blues, easy-listening songs, you name it. Just as he was riveted whenever she played the piano with the skill of a classical pianist. Together, they made sweet music in more ways than one.

Till the music died, seemingly before they ever knew what hit them.

Restarting it together would be a dream come true.

Or were some dreams simply out of reach with the baggage of time gone by?

Landon took another sip of the beer, then walked toward the sliding glass door to the balcony and gazed out. It offered a nice view of the downtown area. That was great, but it was not half as nice as what he saw outside from the vantage point of the house he once shared with Raquelle. When the marriage ended, he didn't hesitate for even a moment to turn over the property to her lock, stock, and barrel. He saw no reason to take away something special that they both had wanted. Even if he would no longer be around to enjoy it. He owed Raquelle that much. And probably a lot more.

If the opportunity ever arises to try and make it up to her, I'll take it, Landon told himself, tasting more beer.

In the meantime, there was the major issue of her brother missing, his prized boat totally destroyed. The big question remained as to whether or not he had been killed by someone who discovered he was helping the feds and was determined to stop him dead in his tracks.

Landon pondered this as he finished off the beer and then headed upstairs to take a shower before having something to eat.

Chapter Four

The following morning, Landon stood in a conference room at the Bureau's field office on Caughman Farm Lane. He was holding an Art Crime Team briefing on the situation pertaining to Eddie and the investigation underway. Sitting in brown PU leather chairs around a black rectangle table were Katie Kitagawa and Special Agent in Charge Shannon Whitfield. Forty-five, long-legged and shapely, with blue eyes and a sandy-colored jellyfish blunt haircut, she was on her second round of running the FBI Columbian field office after being transferred back there seven months ago from the FBI field office in Albuquerque, New Mexico.

Standing was Special Agent Zach Fajardo, who worked within the Transnational Organized Crime division. Hispanic, short, and solidly built, and on his second marriage, he was pushing forty but looked younger, with black hair in a fade crew cut, brown eyes, and a chevron mustache. His focus was primarily on the Racketeer Influenced and Corrupt Organizations Act, or RICO provisions, criminally and civilly, of the laws pertaining to TOC groups and individuals.

Lifting a stylus pen to the large multi-touch monitor, Landon wasted no time in getting to the heart of the matter as he put Eddie's picture on the screen and said in a serious tone, "Eddie Jernigan is my CHS." No reason to reiterate their relationship by marriage as his onetime brother-in-law. "Yesterday, Jernigan's Crest Savannah 250 SLSC pontoon boat was blown up at the Knotter Marina. According to the ATF explosives officer, Chelsea Furillo, an IED was used to carry out the attack. Eddie wasn't on the boat when the explosion occurred, but he's missing. A search by divers in the lake came up empty. But Eddie's apartment was ransacked, indicating that whoever set off the bomb remotely was also looking for something, likely incriminating—and they may or may not have found it."

Shannon clasped her hands and asked, "And you think this is related to your investigation?"

"I'm pretty sure it is," he answered matter-of-factly. "Prior to the bombing, Eddie left me a voicemail, indicating that he was certain they were onto him as my CI and believed that he was in trouble on the boat. By the time I got there, it was on fire—what was left of it—and Eddie was nowhere to be found." Landon took a breath. "His personal and burner cell phones have gone dead," he added, definitely no pun intended, even if the eerie parallels to Eddie's absence went without saying.

Katie leaned forward and asked, "What about the person spotted fleeing the scene, seemingly in a hurry?"

"Definitely a person of interest," Landon told her candidly and put an image on the monitor. "A surveillance camera picked up the unsub near the marina store. Can't get a good read on him, with a hood over the head and half facing away from the camera—we're trying to line this up with other video footage—but we believe the suspect is a tall white male with black or brown hair, probably in his thirties or forties. And he may be driving a white Hyundai Santa Fe SUV or a silver Honda Accord. A BOLO has been issued for both vehicles."

"Any word on Jernigan's vehicle?" Shannon asked interestedly.

"Yeah." Landon's inflection dropped an octave as he switched images on the monitor. "Eddie's white Audi Q4 Sportback e-tron was picked up by a Flock camera an hour after the explosion as it crossed Eighth Street and Ropper Road. The license plate reader couldn't make out the driver, which may or may not have been Jernigan. The car was found abandoned near a farmhouse three miles away. Witnesses reported an adult man wearing a hoodie running away from the scene, but no positive identification has been made."

"So, if Jernigan was the driver," Zach put forth, "then he may have hitched a ride with someone else. Or stolen another car to get away."

He shook his head to both suggestions. "There are no reports of any stolen vehicles in the area," he pointed out, while keeping an open mind that the unidentified driver could have been Raquelle's brother. "Eddie's vehicle is being examined for DNA and dusted for prints. As far as hitching a ride, I doubt that he was making a concerted effort to drag someone else into this." *Definitely not Raquelle*, Landon told himself, as Eddie had apparently made no attempt to contact her since he went missing. It was as though he was unable to—more than unwilling to—which concerned Landon in and of itself. "I also can't rule out that Eddie could have been kidnapped and is being held against his will in either seeking to gain intel from him or as a bargaining chip down the line…"

Shannon asked, "So, where do things stand in the investigation, with the CI strangely absent from the picture—dead or alive, abducted or not—as it relates to the case?"

Landon had anticipated the question and contemplated a response. "The case is still continuing and moving in the right direction," he said levelly. "Eddie was supplying useful intel in building a solid case against forty-seven-year-old art dealer Ivan Pimentel." Landon put the image of the suspect on the screen. He had an oval face, blue eyes, and bleached hair in a long quiff and a Van Dyke beard. "Pimentel has a number of art galleries throughout South Carolina, including several in and around Columbia, one in Charleston, another in Summerville. He also owns a gallery in Miami, Florida, and another in London, England. We believe that Pimentel is using the art galleries to buy and sell both stolen and forged works of Native American art and laundering the significant proceeds from it, while defrauding some unsuspected buyers and working hand in hand with others knowingly. His criminal enterprise has international ties in conspiring with others to commit art and cultural property crimes."

Zach jutted his chin and said in an almost giddy yet serious tone of voice, "If played right, the RICO charges—such as conspiracy to commit art theft or steal and dispose of pieces of cultural heritage, forgery, money laundering, bank, mail and wire fraud, aggravated identity theft, and interstate or international transportation of stolen property—will blow this illegal operation wide open."

"It could at that," Landon acknowledged.

"We get it." Katie laughed. "Calm down, Fajardo. It's still a work in progress."

"I'm just saying," he voiced with a chuckle.

Shannon pursed her lips while peering at Landon. "Do you have enough to make arrests that can stick—with or without Jernigan's cooperation?" the special agent in charge asked pointedly.

"Yes and no." He hoped to buy more time. "We can certainly make a strong case against Pimentel and his associates as is. But I'd still like to dig in a little deeper to truly tighten the screws on his criminal network. Moreover, if Pimentel was involved in Eddie's disappearance and bombing of his boat, along with burglarizing his apartment—which I believe is a strong possibility—then we'd have even more serious offenses we can hang on him."

"Makes sense." Shannon ran a hand through her hair. "But not enough to drag this thing out for who knows how long. Especially if your CHS isn't available to provide useful intel."

"About that…" Landon pressed a hand flat on the conference table. "Actually, I was thinking of going undercover myself as an art collector to try and get more incriminating evidence of stolen or phony works of art from Pimentel." *It sounds like a good idea anyway, while also getting a read on the circumstances surrounding Eddie's disappearance*, he told himself, watching everyone's surprised reaction. Especially Shannon's look of shock.

The special agent in charge furrowed her brow. "Not sure that works for me," she said boldly. "It was one thing to convince Eddie Jernigan to be an inside source of info, but given your personal connection to him, throwing caution to the wind by going in and assuming he hasn't already spilled his guts to the other side doesn't make sense. And it could jeopardize the investigation."

Though he fully understood her point of view and didn't necessarily disagree, Landon pushed back nevertheless. "I wouldn't exactly be throwing caution to the wind," he insisted. "I would take precautions and focus on identifying some specific Native American art that was stolen or faked—to label as evidence of criminality."

Shannon wasn't buying it as she responded steadfastly, "I'd rather keep you on the outside in this instance." She eyed Katie and Zach. "On the other hand, if you'd still like to dig a bit more surreptitiously, I say we have Special Agents Kitagawa and Fajardo go undercover, posing as a couple who's interested in Native American art as part of their broader art collection."

Just as Zach started to protest, Katie said swiftly, "I'm game. As an Indigenous Hawaiian, and just as keen on preserving our culture through art, artifacts, and other means as Native Americans are, I can definitely pull this off on my end."

With all eyes now on Zach, he relented, acquiescing, "If Katie is willing to jump into the ring on this, count me in."

Shannon smiled softly. "Then it's settled."

This should be interesting, Landon thought with amusement, knowing that both Katie and Zach were in serious relationships in their real lives. *I only wish I could say the same,* he told himself, but he said out loud, "We'll make it work."

"If you say so," Katie quipped, adding, "Whatever it takes to reach the ultimate goal of taking down Ivan Pimentel and his associates."

Zach said, "Agreed."

"To that point," Shannon voiced as she stood up in her

dark-colored windowpane pantsuit and peered at Landon, "Agent Briscoe, you need to find out, one way or another, if Eddie Jernigan is still a CHS. If not—because he's deceased, held in captivity, or freely chosen to go underground—we have to know if he left behind valuable intel that can move this investigation along."

Landon nodded respectfully. "I understand." The show had to go on, whether Raquelle's brother was still among the living or not. *I owe it to her to see to it that Eddie did not die in vain, if that's the outcome*, he thought. And if his previous brother-in-law was in possession of more damaging evidence that could be used against Pimentel and was still accessible to the Art Crime Team, he needed that information.

As the briefing ended, Landon turned his thoughts to Raquelle, wondering where they might go from here. Along with if Eddie could, against the odds, still be around to reach out to her—and himself.

RAQUELLE STOOD IN the Hubley Auditorium, where she was the project director for a Department of Theatre student production. She watched as the students—all vying for their bachelor of fine arts in acting for the stage and screen—went through rehearsals for the contemporary drama.

Though she was largely ensconced in providing the guidance needed for a successful production, Raquelle was admittedly unable to keep from breaking away mentally from the student performances as her mind wandered back and forth between her brother and ex-husband. She had yet to hear from Eddie but refused to give up hope that he could still come out of this somehow, without the worst-case scenario.

But how would things emerge with Landon? Would they be able to get past their differences and find common ground in reestablishing a relationship of some kind? Or had his reemergence in her life been more about dealing with his CI than repairing what was once a strong partnership in marriage?

I need to chill out, Raquelle admonished herself as she trained her eyes on the actors on stage, working in harmony. Forcing her mind to churn overtime was not helpful to herself. Eddie. Or even Landon.

At least she had a means of escape in her role as a professor in the theater department through various productions that provided students valuable learning experience.

When her cell phone vibrated, Raquelle pulled it from the side pocket of her white linen crop pants and saw that it was a text message from Landon, asking her, Are you free for lunch?

She texted him back, Yes, where?

He suggested a café called Joslyn's Place not far from the college, and she agreed, then the text exchange ended abruptly.

Raquelle tried not to read anything into that but was eager for any news on Eddie as she refocused on the stage production.

When it was over and she was about to head out, one of the students, Vera Mahaffey, approached her. The twenty-four-year-old graduate teaching assistant and costume designer for the performance was petite and had curly red hair in a U-cut. Vera was wearing horn-shaped glasses, which she pushed up before saying anxiously, "Professor

Jernigan, I thought you should know that when I parked, I saw a man snooping around your car in the lot—"

"Really?" Raquelle cocked a brow. *Could it have been Eddie?* she mused. "Did you get a good look at the person?"

"Afraid not." Vera frowned. "He had a hood over his head and was wearing somewhat baggy clothing. When he saw me, he just took off running—and disappeared on campus."

"Hmm." She thought about the man she had seen moving rapidly at the marina, just before Eddie's boat exploded. Was this the same person? If so, how would he know where she worked? Or what type of car she drove? *On the other hand, Eddie knew both*, Raquelle told herself musingly.

When she stepped outside, Raquelle was leery and on guard as she headed toward the parking lot. Her eyes scanned it, looking for any sign that she was being followed or watched. She had hoped that she would see Eddie, coming to her for help out of his current predicament. At least she would know that he was alive. And they could go from there.

But she did not see her brother, dampening Raquelle's optimism. But there was no indication that another man—perhaps the one fleeing Knotter Marina yesterday—was lurking about her Infiniti Q50 sedan.

Well, that's a relief anyway, she thought and wondered if Vera, who had sometimes been prone to exaggeration since becoming her teaching assistant, had jumped the gun in her assessment of the situation and reaction to the supposed snooper.

After getting into the vehicle and locking the doors,

Raquelle checked the surroundings once more before starting up the engine and heading out for her luncheon date with Landon. She certainly didn't look at this as a real date with her ex-husband but found herself looking forward to it nonetheless, if it could lead to a positive outcome for Eddie and his disappearance.

HE WATCHED FROM behind a building, with a bird's-eye view of the lot. Specifically, he was watching as Raquelle Jernigan showed up at the car she drove. He had spotted her at the marina just as he was leaving.

She had seen him, though he seriously doubted that she could pick him out of a lineup, much less recognize him if she passed him on the street. He had been wearing the same hood over his head that he wore now. And had his back to her for the most part.

Still, she was a potential witness. And a possible obstacle in his mission that he might have to deal with.

Just as he had the pontoon boat owned by her brother. The fact that he managed to miraculously escape the explosion meant nothing.

Eddie Jernigan was a dead man walking. And only biding time that he was in very short supply of.

He was sure that the informant knew this as well and would pay dearly for this act of betrayal. It was only a matter of patience and determination before he finished the job he was paid handsomely to do by his employer— eliminating the deceitful art dealer.

Short of that, Eddie's good-looking theater-professor sister was in his crosshairs as a way to draw the snitch out in the open. Or simply eliminate her altogether as partial payment on the life of her brother—till his time was up for good.

He sucked in a deep breath before emerging from the shadows, knowing that Raquelle Jernigan had driven off, no longer able to spot him, only to try and escape. But that would be all but impossible should it come to that.

The clock was ticking for her—much like the bomb he had detonated remotely—almost as quickly as it was for Eddie Jernigan.

He headed toward the parking lot, where his Toyota Tundra pickup awaited. Once inside, he lifted his cell phone and informed his employer about the sister and how he planned to proceed from here.

Chapter Five

Joslyn's Place on Orrin Way was busier with patrons than Landon had expected but was still a good choice to meet with its proximity to Braedon College. For whatever reason, he actually felt butterflies in his stomach at the prospect of having lunch with his ex-wife, as though it was a real date like the first one for them at the University of South Carolina.

Only this *date* was much different, insofar as the circumstances that brought them together again. Landon wondered if Raquelle would have given him the time of day were it not for her obvious concern about Eddie. Had he confided in her before disappearing? Could she have intel that, in the absence of her brother, could still be used against Ivan Pimentel?

Landon came back to Raquelle having given him the cold shoulder ever since the divorce. Or was he overstating things? Fact was she had every right to put family—which he was no longer a part of—first, even taking back her maiden name of Jernigan to put further distance between them.

Even if that hurt more than Landon cared to admit, she was no less guilty than himself for allowing their marriage to fall apart and finding it hard—if not impossible—to pick up the pieces of a fractured relationship. Raquelle owed him nothing and he knew it. To suggest otherwise and want a do-over just might be asking too much.

Keep telling yourself that, Landon contemplated uneasily as he tasted the black coffee while awaiting Raquelle in a booth near the picture window.

When she showed up right on time, he waved her over while wondering if she still played the piano. He could think of no reason why she wouldn't, given the joy it seemed to bring her. Even if his own guitar playing was infrequent these days.

Like a gentleman, Landon stood after Raquelle got to the table and said to her in a friendly tone of voice, "Hey."

"Hey," she responded tentatively and slid into one side of the booth.

Landon sat back on the other side. "I ordered coffee with cream." He eyed the steaming mug in front of her, remembering how she liked her coffee.

Raquelle smiled thinly. "Thanks." She lifted the mug and took a sip, setting it back down as she regarded him. "Do you have any news about Eddie...?"

"We haven't found him yet, if that's what you're asking," Landon wished he didn't have to say. But he tried to get past this obvious disappointment nonetheless—that would likely get worse—while meeting her eyes that were somehow unreadable. "There have been some developments... Why don't we order lunch first?"

She was amenable to this. "Okay."

He picked up the menu, just for effect, having already decided upon the baked whiting fillet, served with hush puppies and steamed vegetables. Raquelle went with the grilled chicken, baked potato, and house salad.

After tasting his coffee, Landon sat back. "It's been

confirmed that an improvised explosive device was detonated remotely on Eddie's pontoon boat. Someone was determined to blow it up—with or without Eddie's presence—and succeeded. Fortunately, no other boats caught fire. Nor were there any reported injuries."

Raquelle frowned. "But Eddie's still missing...?"

"Yes, I'm afraid so." Landon wished that weren't the case, for more reasons than the most important one—his life. "His Audi was found abandoned on Piliford Lane. A man wearing a hoodie was seen leaving the scene. We're still reviewing surveillance video in the area to try and identify him—but given the fact that Eddie has not surfaced, there's a strong possibility that he wasn't the one who ditched the car."

"Hmm..." Raquelle gave him a thoughtful look. "My GTA told me that a hooded man wearing baggy clothing was seen prowling around my car in the lot at Braedon College—before disappearing on campus when spotted. I was thinking that it could have been Eddie—running scared and looking for somewhere to turn..."

"Possible," Landon allowed musingly. If her brother was still alive, it would be natural that he would reach out to her, if desperate enough. But there was an alternative explanation on the unsub. "If it was Eddie, he made no attempt to hang around long enough to hitch a ride with you. Based on the description of the snooper, sounds a lot like the man you saw leaving Knotter Marina prior to the boat explosion."

Raquelle sipped more coffee. "Yes, I thought about that too," she conceded. "If so, why would he have been snooping around my car? How would he even know I worked at the college?"

As Landon watched the uneasiness sweep across her face like a shadow, he responded candidly, "If Eddie was indeed the intended target of the boat explosion—but survived—the perpetrator likely had enough intel to know about you and may simply have been fishing, in search of Eddie." *I hope it doesn't go any deeper than that*, he told himself while hoping that campus surveillance video could pinpoint the person and where he might have gone. What if the unsub feared being identified by her? Based on what Raquelle said she saw of the possible bomber, it didn't appear as though she would be able to finger him. She would still need to watch her back and Landon told her so, to be on the safe side. "Be extra vigilant on campus and off. If you see this man again—or think you see him—let me know."

Raquelle heeded this warning but said bluntly, "Right now, I'm more concerned about Eddie's health and well-being. What exactly are you doing to find him? If he's still alive, how do you plan to keep my brother safe?"

Two big questions that deserved responsible answers. Landon wanted to give them to her to the best of his ability but was glad that the food arrived. It bought him a little time to contemplate how best to respond, while hoping to temper her expectations.

RAQUELLE STARED AT Landon over her food, waiting for a response to her concerns about Eddie. If he was on the lam in fear of his life, she certainly wanted the authorities to find him before whoever it was that wanted Eddie dead did. She assumed Landon felt the same way—even if his motives may have differed from hers as an FBI agent, considering that Eddie was working for him as a CI before he went missing.

After slicing a fork into his whiting fillet, Landon looked at her and said coolly, "Right now, Eddie's still considered a missing person. This includes a possible abduction. To that end, the Falona County Sheriff's Office has been notified. They have personnel from the Special Victims Unit's Missing Persons team searching for him. Same is true for the Gadwall Heights Police Department, after Eddie's apartment was broken into in their jurisdiction, in relation to his disappearance."

That's something, Raquelle told herself, giving her hope that Eddie was hiding and not a kidnapping or, worse, homicide victim. She peered at Landon and forked a piece of lettuce from her house salad, then repeated her question intently, "And what is the FBI doing to locate and protect Eddie?"

Landon swallowed food before dabbing a napkin on his lips and insisting, "Everything we can. As a confidential human source for a federal investigation by the Art Crime Team, Eddie's disappearance under suspicious circumstances has the Bureau's attention. Apart from agents working with local law enforcement to try and find him— including dispatching a search and rescue team and K-9 unit to search in and around the wooded area near Eddie's apartment complex—the info has been put into the FBI's National Crime Information Center and Violent Criminal Apprehension Program. Both are repositories for major cases, which include info on missing persons in relation to acts of violence, such as the bombing of a boat.

"Similarly," he pointed out while scooping up some hush puppies, "the South Carolina Law Enforcement Division's Missing Person Information Center has also been alerted, along with the Tribal Access Program—in case we need to exchange info that could lead to finding or identifying Eddie."

"All right," Raquelle said, digging her fork into the baked potato while feeling reasonably comfortable that they were taking her brother's disappearance seriously.

Landon seemed to read into her thoughts as he forked a steamed carrot. Meeting her gaze, he said, "Just so you know, I'm just as concerned for Eddie's safety as you are, Raquelle. Aside from being a confidential human source, he's still my brother-in-law—more or less—and I actually consider him to be a friend, strange as that may seem…"

It does sound weird in a way but believable in another, she told herself, knowing the character of both men. Even if they were so different and—as it turned out—apparently on opposite sides of the law.

She looked at her ex. "Thank you for saying that," she said sincerely. "These days, especially since the breakup with his last girlfriend, Eddie hasn't quite seemed himself." If she was being honest about it, though, Raquelle realized now that he had more than one thing on his mind. "Having someone he looked up to as a confidant—even if it was for investigative purposes—was probably good for him." She frowned thoughtfully. "Till it wasn't."

Landon acknowledged this while pinching the bridge his nose, musing. "About that…" He held her gaze unwaveringly. "I need to know if Eddie talked to you about his recent dealings in the art world…"

"Not really." Raquelle's eyes grew wide. She sensed that he was wondering if she knew that Eddie was selling counterfeit art. Or perhaps had some further insight into his activities, legal or not. Her gaze narrowed at Landon, and she said, "I knew, of course, that Eddie fancied himself as a seller of Native American art when he could get his hands on it—but that's about all. He never involved me in any of his dealings, as was Eddie's nature. We pretty much kept our professional lives separate from our personal relationship as siblings."

"Okay—just asking." Landon tasted his coffee, making a face to indicate that it had turned cold. "I wasn't in any way accusing you of anything," he emphasized.

Her lashes fluttered skeptically. "Are you sure about that?"

"Yeah, positive." He reached out and placed a strong hand atop hers. "You're not under investigation, Raquelle, trust me. Neither is Eddie, as things now stand. In his current absence, I only wondered if he might have left you with anything for safe keeping—in case he ran into trouble."

"He didn't," she stressed, sliding her hand from under his and taking a sip of water. "Whatever evidence Eddie might have collected on your behalf, it probably went up in flames on his boat. Or was stolen from his apartment." If her brother was still alive, Raquelle considered that he might have taken evidence with him that could be used as an insurance policy against his life. Or had he reached a point where even if that were the case, Eddie didn't know who he could trust? Did that include Landon?

"You're probably right," he told her, a catch to his voice. "Just know that however this turns out, I'm on your side. Never stopped."

That was news to her, but Raquelle felt this wasn't the time or place to delve into their failed marriage. Meanwhile, she was glad they were on the same team, as near as she could establish, where it concerned wanting Eddie back alive and well. Even if Landon's motivations had to be related to his investigation into art crime and the important role her brother played in solving the case.

THAT AFTERNOON, LANDON WAS in his car en route to an appraiser of Native American art and artifacts in downtown Columbia, seeking to determine the authenticity of a painting that an art gallery owned by Ivan Pimentel sold online. It was one of many ways that Pimentel did business trying to legitimize art criminality.

But just how far had he gone to protect his interests? And at what cost?

Landon's thoughts turned to Raquelle. He regretted having to question her about Eddie. Worse was any notion she might have that he was accusing her of being a party to her brother's involvement in the art world.

The last thing Landon wanted was to put any further walls between them. Just the opposite. He wanted more than anything to break down the barriers that had torn them apart. But there was still the matter of Eddie's whereabouts—dead or alive. And Landon's own role in recruiting his former brother-in-law as a CHS. He was obligated to get to the bottom of Eddie's disappearance and continue to work on the case, wherever it led.

Surely Raquelle, as the former wife of an FBI special agent gets that—right? Landon told himself as he pulled into the parking lot slot on Taylor Street. How could she not? But he completely understood that, at the moment, her loyalty was to her brother—and having the best-case scenario emerge as to his disposition, current and future.

Exiting the car, Landon took a quick look at his cell phone, where there was a text from Shannon Whitfield. The special agent in charge was simply updating him on funds being approved and allocated for Katie and Zach's undercover assignment, if needed, in further exposing Ivan Pimentel as an art thief.

After texting her back with his satisfaction, Landon headed into the studio of Brenda Hatcher, an FBI consultant on art and artifacts criminality.

Brenda was Native American and in her fifties. Short and slender, with brunette hair in a pixie cut, she greeted him with a handshake and said evenly, "Agent Briscoe."

Landon smiled softly. "So, what have you learned?" he asked eagerly, glancing about the studio that had various works of art on the floor against the wall and on wooden tables. There was also a workstation standing desk. He homed in on an oil painting on a table. It was of early Native Americans settled on the banks of the Wateree River. The name derived from the Wateree tribe of Native Americans that originated in the Carolinas in the sixteenth century. It was purportedly an original painting by the early nineteenth-century artist Eva Helen Würdemann that Pimentel sold unknowingly to the FBI for a pretty penny.

Brenda looked Landon right in the eye and said succinctly, "It's a fake!"

"Really?" He acted surprised but wasn't really, having suspected as much. "Tell me more."

"All right." They walked over to the painting, where she donned a pair of impermeable nitrile gloves from the table. She lifted up the painting and, pointing at the signature, said, "For one, the signature is not consistent with Ms. Würdemann's, either in placement or the particulars, in accordance with other paintings by the artist. A forensic handwriting expert I employ, Geoff Crisologo, confirmed that the signature on this painting was bogus."

"Hmm, okay," Landon said, regarding the fraudulent work of art. "What else?"

"Chemical testing of the painting showed that there were titanium pigments included, which didn't come till years after the Eva Würdemann painting was completed." Brenda held it at an angle. "Beyond that, subtle—but significant nonetheless to a trained eye—differences in layering, coloring, and texture illustrate that this so-called original work of art has been copied, and poorly at that."

"I see." He fixed her face. "And the real painting by Eva Helen Würdemann?" he asked probingly.

Brenda licked her lips. "It's safely and legitimately on display at the Smithsonian Institution's National Museum of the American Indian on the National Mall in Washington, DC."

"Good." Landon grinned, satisfied. Another nail in Ivan Pimentel's proverbial coffin. "I'll be taking the phony painting with me."

She smiled. "It's all yours."

Landon took the painting to the field office and logged it in the evidence room. He conferred briefly with Shannon and Katie. Both agreed that the counterfeit painting was another important step in the investigation with more tightening of the screws against Pimentel, minus Eddie's absence in the scheme of things.

On the way home, Landon stopped at Lee's Cuisine, a Chinese restaurant in Lexington on Quallford Lane, for takeout of fried shrimp and beef egg rolls.

He sat in the built-in kitchen booth, downing the food with water. Another day in time where loneliness ate away at him like a cancer. Yes, he was used to the routine and didn't always have reason to complain. But spending time with Raquelle again had reminded him what he was missing, and would love to have back in his life again: a relationship with substance.

After eating and pouring himself a glass of wine, Landon gave Raquelle a call. He wasn't sure what he would say. Only that he wanted to hear the sound of her voice, one that had enticed him from the first time it reached his ears.

When she picked up, he said casually, "Hey."

"Hey." She had that nice ring to her inflection. "What's up?" she asked, clearly anticipating that he had something to report on Eddie's disappearance, good or bad.

I have neither to report, Landon thought with regret. "Just wanted to check on you," he said in what amounted to a half truth.

"I'm fine," Raquelle stated. "My back feels a little stiff, which happens every now and then for whatever reason."

"I remember," he told her, along with his being there to give her a nice back rub. It often seemed to do the trick.

"It'll pass," she said, as if reading his mind. "Anything on Eddie?"

"Still searching for him." Landon knew that wasn't what she wanted to hear. "No news is good news, right?" he told her as a way to not give up on the possibility that Eddie could still be alive—somewhere.

"I suppose." Raquelle paused. "He's not a quitter. If there's any way—"

Landon only wondered if there was a way for Eddie to beat back the odds and come out of this whole. "I agree." He strove to maintain a positive attitude while being realistic as well.

"How's your mom?" Raquelle broke into his thoughts.

"She's good." Landon recalled that his mother and

Raquelle got along nicely during the marriage, each respecting the other. But as one would expect, after the divorce, they pretty much drifted apart socially—just as he and Raquelle had. "Mom met a man on a dating site last year, and they got married six months ago."

"How nice," Raquelle cadenced. "I'm happy for her—them."

"Me too. Though I have to admit it's still a bit hard getting used to her now being Mrs. Chuck Pritchard."

"You'd better." She chuckled. "Practice makes perfect."

"True." Landon only wished their own marriage had not fallen apart. But it seemed like the only option at the time. Was it?

Raquelle said thoughtfully, "I should go."

"Okay." He enjoyed talking to her, however brief. "I'll be in touch," he told her, wanting to say more but leaving that door open for now.

"Bye." She disconnected.

Landon went into the living room, grabbed his guitar, and sat on an accent chair. He began to play it, while imagining Raquelle playing the piano alongside him in a soulful duet of sounds. Maybe they could still recreate the music that was once such a big part of their lives.

Or at least work their way back toward the passions they shared.

But first, the matter of Eddie's vanishing act still needed to be resolved, knowing that Raquelle was unlikely to think in terms of moving forward with her own life until she got some answers.

Chapter Six

Raquelle accepted Eddie's invitation to have lunch with him aboard his Crest Savannah 250 SLSC pontoon. He warned her it wasn't anything special. Just ham sandwiches, potato chips, oatmeal cookies, and beer or wine—her choice.

As it was, she didn't need anything special. Apart from being open-minded with food, she was happy to spend time with her brother—something that had become less and less frequent in recent times because of their busy schedules. But with no other living relatives, Raquelle was determined not to let her relationship with Eddie fall by the wayside.

Not if she could help it.

So she drove to the marina, exuberant and ready to dine, laugh, reminisce about their childhood when both had such fun but couldn't wait to grow up—and even try to break down where things went wrong in their failed relationships.

As far as Raquelle was concerned, nothing would be off limits. She just wanted to be herself and expected the same from Eddie.

When she arrived at Knotter Marina, Raquelle routinely left her car and headed for the walkway. She nearly *bumped into a tall man wearing a hooded sweatshirt, dark jeans, and dark running shoes. The hood was covering his head. He glared at her with dark eyes but said nothing.*

Neither did she as he quickly walked away as though late for an appointment.

Raquelle turned from the man and resumed moving across the dock toward her brother's boat. She glanced nonchalantly at the rude man who almost bowled her over and saw him look back at her, as if sensing she was looking, before vanishing from sight. Refocusing, she gave a sweeping scan of the other boats docked on opposite sides of Eddie's pontoon.

Just as she got within a few feet of it, Raquelle saw Eddie on board waving at her, grinning cheerfully while inviting her to climb aboard. She giggled while accepting the invitation.

But before she was able to take another step, the pontoon suddenly exploded into flames. She watched in horror as her brother was being burned alive, his screams excruciating to hear.

Feeling an overwhelming urge to help him, Raquelle started to race toward the boat while crying out for help. Before she could get there, powerful arms held her back, against her wishes. Unable to break free, she twisted her neck and locked eyes with her ex-husband.

As determined as she was to save her brother, Landon was just as driven in preventing her from burning to death too.

When she looked back to the boat that was totally engulfed in a ball of fire and fury, Raquelle screamed as though she were being consumed by the fire.

RAQUELLE HEARD MOANS coming from her mouth as she opened her eyes. It took her a few moments to adjust to the darkness in the wee hours of Saturday morning to grasp that she was in her rustic platform queen bed. The terrifying experience was only a nightmare. *None of it was real, thankfully*, she thought. Not that it took away from the reality that Eddie's boat was bombed and that he was probably supposed to be on it. But he wasn't. It gave her something to hold on to.

He might still be alive. And not physically harmed.

Dragging herself out from beneath the cotton sheet, Raquelle realized that her silk chemise was wet from perspiration. She wasn't surprised that her body temperature had risen when being hit with such an awful dream. *I'm glad that Landon was there, like in real life, to prevent me from jumping into the fire and perishing*, she told herself. She only wished he had been there for her before their marriage went sour. Or was that being totally unfair to him? Neither had necessarily seen what was coming to somehow prevent things from playing out as they had.

After removing the chemise and tossing it into the washer, Raquelle dried herself and slipped into a short, knit nightgown. She padded barefoot down the stairs and grabbed a bottled water from the refrigerator, downing half of it.

She heard the floor creak and thought that someone might be inside the house. Eddie? Or had the man who hovered around her car—and might have set off the bomb on Eddie's boat—found out where she lived?

"Eddie...?" Raquelle called out tentatively. No response. She tried again. No answer.

Her first instinct was to call Landon and report a possible break-in. But was that really necessary? Was it a smart idea to allow herself to become dependent on her ex-husband, who likely had someone else in his life these days?

There were no more sounds, and Raquelle now suspected that the creaking was nothing more than the typical noise she had grown accustomed to since moving to the house. Couple that with still feeling jittery after the nightmare and she could see how easy it was to be spooked.

She went back upstairs to bed, while wondering if there was any way she could go back to sleep—given the confluence of Eddie and Landon playing with her mind tremulously.

KATIE KITAGAWA HAD no doubt that they could pull this off as she rode alongside Zach Fajardo in his gray Chevy Tahoe SUV. Though she was ten years his junior and they weren't a match made in heaven—unlike with her real partner in romance, Tony Razo, or for that matter, Zach and his wife, Celeste—they got along well, and Katie saw no reason why they couldn't walk into that art gallery owned by Ivan Pimentel and convincingly pretend to be a couple fascinated by Native American art. Never mind that undercover work wasn't exactly either of their forte as FBI special agents—desperate times called for desperate measures. Or at least it felt as though they needed to step up and do their parts to build the case against the suspected international art lawbreaker. Particularly with Landon's CI, Eddie Jernigan, inaccessible and probably in serious trouble.

With or without Jernigan, we still have a job to do,

Katie told herself, while mindful that Landon's relationship with him through his former marriage made the CI's disappearance and possible murder personal as well as business.

"Well, here we are," Zach said concisely as he pulled into the parking lot of the Beaks Art Gallery on State Street in West Columbia.

"Here we are," Katie mimicked him lightheartedly, though serious in their mission. The gallery was believed to have been used by Pimentel to sell Native American stolen works of art that would need to be repatriated to their rightful owners. "We'll see if the art gallery has what we're looking for."

"Sounds good, girlfriend, wife, or whatever you wish," he responded playfully.

"Close friends with no benefits," she joked. "But, yes, looking every bit as a couple, to pull this off."

"Got it." He smiled. "And if we spot any of the stolen paintings on our radar, we can take it from there—while watching the federal charges continue to pile up against the crooked art dealer."

Katie added, "Not to mention any other charges that could be forthcoming as it pertains to the missing Eddie Jernigan."

"Yeah, there is that," Zach concurred as they got out of the car.

Dressed in casual attire, the two went inside the art gallery, which was small and cozy. Framed paintings lined the walls with other pieces on display tables.

Katie decided on the spur of the moment to hold Zach's hand—as if they were a couple on full display rather than undercover FBI agents—when they were approached by a fortysomething, thin woman with silver hair in a finger waves style. Her nametag identified her as Lucille Thiessen, a sales associate.

"Welcome to Beaks Art Gallery," she spoke cheerfully.

They acknowledged this coolly, and Katie said, "We spotted the gallery while driving by and thought we'd take a look inside."

"I'm happy you did." Lucille showed her teeth. "Are you interested in anything in particular?"

"As a matter of fact, we are," Zach said, releasing his hand from Katie's. "Can you show us what you have in Native American paintings? It would be great to add a piece to our collection."

"Sure, I can help you with that," she said. "We have some magnificent original works of Native American art, both historical and contemporary, by some wonderful artists."

"That's great," Katie told her, sounding excited but actually intrigued at what they might find.

"Follow me," the sales associate told them.

They did just that, holding hands again for effect, as Katie and Zach were led to a section of the gallery where they were tentatively able to identify at least one stolen painting that they were looking for.

LANDON GOT WORD from Katie that she and Zach had zeroed in on two stolen Native American paintings that Ivan Pimentel had managed to get his hands on, including an early twentieth-century portrait of a woman belonging to the Waccamaw Siouan Indian Tribe of North Carolina and a modern landscape that was painted by renowned Cherokee Nation of Oklahoma artist, Jordana Teehee.

Both works of art would be further evidence used against Pimentel when building the case.

While driving to the suspect's main hub, called the Pimentel Gallery, on Lincoln Street in Columbia, Landon couldn't help but think that they already had enough dirt on Pimentel to put him away for a very long time. But there was still more to be had to put even more pressure on him and his criminal enterprise and associates.

That included tying Pimentel to Eddie's disappearance, which seemed to Landon to be a strong probability. Along with Eddie himself, his laptop was missing. Both Eddie's cell phones last pinged by Knotter Marina— around the time his pontoon exploded from the IED. The lack of communication from his previously dependable CHS was disturbing to Landon, to say the least. He considered that Eddie could have been kidnapped and was being held captive somewhere while being forced to reveal what he had shared with the FBI. Raquelle's brother could also be injured and unable to communicate— assuming he was still alive.

Landon kept all possibilities on the table, in spite of fearing that Eddie was in a place where there was no coming back from—leaving Raquelle to deal with the aftermath.

Arriving at his destination, Landon parked and went inside the art gallery. Impressive in size, it featured various collections and exhibits of artistic expression, both historical and contemporary, for collectors and visitors alike. *How many of the works were forgeries or stolen art?* he wondered, beyond those that the Art Crime Team had already established, as he walked around.

When Landon approached two men standing near a

display of fine art, he recognized one as Ivan Pimentel.
Tall and trim, he was wearing a tailored gray wool suit
and black cap toe Oxford shoes. The other man, one of
Pimentel's cronies—or someone employed to do his dirty
work—was Yusef Abercrombie. Known to the Bureau
with a criminal record, he was younger than Pimentel
and of similar height, in his mid-thirties, and paunch-
ier, with dark hair in a hipster cut and low fade. He had
a full beard.

They stopped talking as Landon walked up to them.
Pimentel looked at him with blue eyes and asked evenly,
"Can I help you?"

Landon met his gaze and said, pretending to be clue-
less, "I'm looking for the owner of the art gallery."

"You found him," he said. "I'm Ivan Pimentel."

Whipping out identification from a pocket of his wool
blend blazer, Landon said measuredly, "FBI Special Agent
Briscoe." He watched as both men reacted to this ill at
ease. "I'd like to ask you some questions pertaining to an
investigation," Landon told Pimentel.

He looked at his associate and said commandingly,
"Give us a moment."

Abercrombie seemed reluctant to leave but acquiesced
to his directive, glaring at Landon before he left them
alone.

Pimentel recovered from his unease. With a thick eye-
brow cocked, he peered at Landon and asked, as if oblivi-
ous, "What's this investigation about, Agent Briscoe?"

*More than I care to fully elaborate on for obvious rea-
sons*, Landon told himself. "We're looking into a boat
explosion at the Knotter Marina. The pontoon belonged
to an art dealer named Eddie Jernigan. He's missing."

"Sorry to hear that." Pimentel rubbed his aquiline nose. "What does it have to do with me?"

"Nothing, I'm sure," Landon lied, but he had to play this the right way for now. "As a routine part of the investigation, we're talking to anyone who Jernigan was associated with—personally and professionally—and might have information on his whereabouts. Or even the boat explosion. That brings me to you as someone we've discovered Jernigan has worked with in buying and selling Native American works of art."

"I've done business with Eddie," Pimentel conceded. "But I know nothing about his boat exploding—or what may have happened to him."

"Too bad." Landon made a face. "As I said, this is standard stuff. If you happen to hear anything about Jernigan's disappearance, let me know." To that end, he took out a card with the appropriate professional contact info for an FBI agent and handed it to Pimentel.

"I'll do that," he promised, glancing at the card and back.

Landon nodded and walked away. *I was afraid Pimentel would go into denial mode*, he told himself while leaving the art gallery. Not that he bought it. Far from it. Pimentel had everything to lose by coming clean about his knowledge of both the bombing of Eddie's pontoon and his mysterious vanishing—including the collapse of Pimentel's criminal enterprise—and everything to gain by lying. At least he was being put on notice while they waited to see what his next move was as the search continued for Eddie. Along with the plan to put an end to Pimentel's art criminality.

IVAN PIMENTEL WATCHED and waited for the FBI special agent to leave, while thinking that the feds were likely onto him and his profitable business of selling genuine and counterfeit artwork, both in the US and abroad. If so, this was thanks in large part of their reliance on Eddie Jernigan. He had trusted Eddie as a reputable and reliable art dealer, helping to facilitate deals worldwide.

Instead, it turned out that the man was a stool pigeon for the feds, passing along info to the FBI that Ivan had no doubt they intended to use against him. But he had been smart enough to limit his exposure, knowing that revealing too much to too many was foolish. Not to mention risky for his own self-interest. That included staying out of prison.

He had removed many of the illicit paintings and artifacts from his galleries and exhibitions—before the feds could confiscate them—and laundered more money to hide from the authorities. Beyond that, he had relied more on private buyers with a stake in the game for financial gain. People who wouldn't be inclined to cooperate with the authorities and spill the beans to their mutual benefit. As well as detriment.

Still, Eddie knew just enough to make him a liability. Ivan was not about to allow the snitch to derail his operation. As far as he was concerned, Eddie was a ticking time bomb, in spite of having apparently survived the boat explosion that was supposed to have him on it as a reward for his betrayal.

Or had he? There was still no sign of Eddie Jernigan. Even the feds and locals had failed to locate the art dealer, though not from lack of trying. This left Ivan to believe that the man hired to kill Jernigan may well have succeeded, but was still holding out. Perhaps to use him as a bargaining chip to extract more money for his services. If so, Ivan would not have it. A deal was a deal. Anything else was pure greed and disloyalty that would need to be dealt with accordingly.

Ivan motioned for Yusef Abercrombie, his right-hand man—who had stayed close by as the FBI special agent asked questions—to return to him, after stepping further away from potentially listening ears of gallery visitors.

Yusef pursed his lips and asked, "What did he want?"

Ivan responded tartly, "To find out if I knew anything about Jernigan's boat blowing up like it did—or Eddie's apparent disappearance."

"And you told the FBI agent?"

"What do you think I told him?" His nostrils flared. "Absolutely nothing."

Yusef looked relieved. "Good."

"Doesn't mean he bought any of it," Ivan argued. "Aside from that, you need to find out from the bomber what the status is of the FBI's CI. If Jernigan's still alive, it had better be just a temporary reprieve. Otherwise, there will be hell to pay—for more people than one," he warned him in no uncertain terms. Yusef's facial expression made it clear to Ivan that he got the message, loud and clear.

"I'll get on it," Yusef assured him. "One way or another, Eddie won't continue to shoot his mouth off to the feds. Trust me, if he hasn't already been taken care of, Eddie's days are numbered."

Favoring him with a hard stare, Ivan said, "That better be the case. Can't have the FBI breathing down my neck—and soon yours to follow."

"I agree." Yusef tugged on his beard. "You don't have to worry."

Ivan gave a nod, eyes narrowed. "So go," he ordered him impatiently.

He watched as Yusef walked away, while taking out his cell phone. As far as Ivan was concerned, once the bomber had verified completing the job, he too then became a liability. And would need to be dealt with the same way as Eddie—so neither of them could come back to haunt him.

Chapter Seven

After a mostly restless sleep, which thankfully didn't come with another nightmare, Raquelle gave up after a while. She got up early, put her hair in a high ponytail, and, to get her weekend off to a good start, went for a run along the wooded trail on the property she once shared with Landon. Wearing brown knit pocket joggers, a pink crop tank, and white running shoes, she made her way through the loblolly pine and southern red oaks, remembering when she used to jog with Landon. Each pushed the other, giving them both a good workout. Then it all ended.

Honestly, she missed those days. But had conditioned herself to accept that some things weren't meant to be. Or was it possible to turn back the clock—or even reset it to a new place in time—where it concerned romance? She thought about Landon's mother finding love again later in life. Anything was possible, right?

Maybe not everything, Raquelle told herself pessimistically. Maybe things with Landon were best left in the past and thinking otherwise could be dangerous.

She thought about Eddie and the danger he faced— assuming he was still out there somewhere alive. And not put out of commission. Or unable to ever be found. Isn't that what people associated with organized crime did to those they wanted rid of: made sure the body would never show up and lead back to them through DNA, prints, or other clues?

I'll never give up on him as long as there's still hope that he can get through the troubles that led to his part-nering up with Landon and becoming his CI, Raquelle thought as she started to jog back to the house. She couldn't help but wonder if Eddie might have turned to his ex-girlfriend, Penelope Dunlap, for a place to hide out. Though their relationship had ended badly, Raquelle be-lieved that her brother still carried a torch for her—and maybe Penelope for him as well. If so, it could be refuge that his pursuers might never be privy to.

With Eddie still officially missing and Landon seem-ingly no closer to getting a handle on where he could be—and with whom—Raquelle thought it incumbent upon her to pay Penelope a visit.

Worth a try, she told herself, returning home. She took a shower, dressed, and had a bowl of cereal for breakfast and a cup of coffee before heading out.

HE WATCHED THROUGH the woods, using high-powered bin-oculars as he surveyed the house that Raquelle Jernigan lived in. She'd just finished jogging, and he had stayed a safe distance away but kept her in sight. The fact that she was Eddie Jernigan's only living relative in the vicin-ity and someone whom Eddie might turn to for his very survival was of interest.

Of less concern at the moment was whether or not Raquelle could actually finger him as the man who'd planted a bomb inside Eddie's boat and detonated it. He realized that his employer would not take kindly to the art professor identifying him, threatening his employer's lucrative art empire. Never mind the personal stakes for continuing to ply his trade uninterrupted by a long stint in prison.

As it was, he was confident that Eddie's sister could no more identify and hand him over to the authorities than she could any other male who happened to be at the marina that day. But Eddie Jernigan was another matter entirely—had her brother managed to survive another brush with death. He'd gunned down someone who fit Eddie's description in the woods near the snitch's apartment complex. But before he could verify that the job had been completed, voices in the area forced him to abandon the mission out of an abundance of caution and self-preservation.

Now he could only wait and see.

He continued watching the house through the binoculars, noting that Raquelle was leaving and getting in her car. No need to follow her. If the circumstances warranted taking her out, he knew right where to find her.

But for now, his only real concern was to make sure that Eddie Jernigan could no longer pass info to the FBI— or stay alive to talk about it with his sister or anyone else.

RAQUELLE ARRIVED AT the Loganfield Hills Condominiums complex on Elkeer Road in Chetlin Bay, a suburb of Columbia and a short drive from Dryer Woods. She'd accompanied Eddie there a couple of times when he and Penelope were still going strong. At the time, Raquelle thought she seemed like a good match for her brother.

Guess I was no better able to judge their romance

surviving than my own, she told herself, reflecting on a marriage that somehow managed to get away from her and Landon.

Raquelle had texted Penelope as a heads-up that she wanted to drop by, while also serving as a message to Eddie to stay put, if she'd allowed him to take shelter there with an X on his back. As Penelope made no attempt to dissuade her, Raquelle could only hope that, at the very least, Eddie had contacted his ex-girlfriend to let her know he was all right.

Which is all I need to hold on to for now, Raquelle told herself. And to pass the information along to Landon.

She knocked on the door of the condo, wondering if Eddie would actually be the one standing there when it opened.

Instead, it was Penelope. In her early thirties, she was attractive and slender, with hazel eyes and long brown hair in multiple layers. An archaeologist, Penelope was a member of the Wassamasaw Tribe of Varnertown Indians with headquarters in Berkeley County, South Carolina.

"Hi," she said in a muted tone.

"Hi." Raquelle gave her a soft smile and was invited inside. She took a glance around the small and neat setting with an open concept on vinyl plank flooring, with lots of windows and midcentury modern furniture. The hope that Eddie would emerge from a bedroom crossed her mind, but it didn't happen. "Nice to see you again, Penelope," she told her, regretting that they had lost touch since the breakup with Eddie.

"You too." Penelope smiled. "Do you want to sit down?"

They sat in caramel faux-leather armchairs, and Raquelle

got right to the point of the visit. "Eddie's gone missing… after his boat exploded—"

Penelope tucked her hair behind an ear and said, "I heard about that…and couldn't believe it."

"I was wondering if he might have come here as a safe haven." Raquelle spoke straightforwardly, again scanning the place. "I know you two weren't seeing each other, but—"

"Eddie's not here," the other woman said succinctly. "I wish he had come to me for help—not that I could've done much. Other than strongly suggest he go to the authorities." She sucked in a deep breath. "But Eddie did call me about a week ago…"

"Really?" Raquelle regarded her. "What did he say?"

"That he had gotten into some trouble—without elaborating. When I asked him what kind of trouble, all Eddie would say was that it involved crooks in the art world and that he was trying to do the right thing by stopping them." She paused. "I wasn't sure exactly what he had in mind and never got the chance to ask, as we were disconnected. I've been unable to reach him since then."

Raquelle told her, figuring she had a right to know and wouldn't likely tell anyone else, "Eddie was working with the FBI."

"Seriously?" Penelope uttered.

"Yes, he was supplying them—actually, my ex-husband, who's a special agent for their Art Crime Team—with info regarding the theft and forgery of Native American art," she revealed, sighing. "It may have cost Eddie his life. We don't know, as he's either gone underground…or they killed him and buried his body somewhere yet to be discovered."

Penelope recoiled at the thought, sharing Raquelle's distress at the prospect, and said in earnest, "I'm so sorry about all of this. Eddie and I may have been a bad fit—or not—but no one should have to go through what he's gotten himself into. Let's hope he's somewhere safe from harm while he tries to figure things out."

"Right," she concurred. "Once we have solid answers, I'll let you know."

"Please do," Penelope insisted.

Raquelle rose and said, "If, by chance, Eddie contacts you again—"

"I'll pass that onto you," she promised, walking her to the door.

Raquelle gave her a hug, knowing Penelope still cared for Eddie and wanted whatever was in his best interests—starting with surviving his current tribulation.

Back in her car, Raquelle pondered both Eddie's disappearance and Landon's efforts to locate him and complete the investigation—while wondering if it was possible that she and Landon could resolve their differences and find a way forward.

LANDON WAS STANDING with Katie in the conference room, studying the big-screen surveillance video from around Knotter Marina. It appeared to show Eddie making a hasty retreat from his Crest Savannah 250 SLSC shortly before it exploded. If nothing else, this told Landon that Eddie had successfully escaped the inferno. But to where? Another place to hide in plain sight, before being taken out?

Looking at the screen, Katie remarked, "The man wearing a hood over his head seemed to just miss Eddie—

and presumably assumed he was still on the boat, when the unsub apparently used a remote-controlled bomb trigger to detonate the IED."

"Yeah, lucky Eddie," Landon spoke with deadpan humor at his brush with being blown to bits. Still, he knew full well that Raquelle's brother had been anything but lucky. Eddie had lost his prized pontoon, for one. Had blown working undercover as an FBI CHS. Had upended the relative calm in Raquelle's world as a theater professor. And now Eddie may well have been tracked down and the hit carried out on his life. "Maybe not so much," Landon entertained ill at ease.

"I wouldn't give up on him just yet," Katie said as she used the stylus to switch to other surveillance videos not far from Eddie's apartment complex in Gadwall Heights and elsewhere in Falona County that showed images of someone who fit Eddie's general description, if not a positive match. "Your CI could well be on the move, while trying to dodge Ivan Pimentel and his goons."

"True," Landon allowed, while still feeling uneasy. "Or we could be on a wild goose chase—considering we've been unable to make contact with Eddie and his known cell phones continue to be inoperative. Does that sound like a man who is alive and wants to stay that way to you?"

Would Eddie keep Raquelle in the dark, not knowing if she should be greeting him with open arms or preparing for his funeral? he asked himself skeptically.

Katie fixed her eyes on his face. "Maybe Eddie wisely ditched his main cell phone and burner phone for fear that either one could lead his pursuers to him as easily as you. All I know is that as long as there's no body, there's no

victim per se. But we do have a suspect—" she brought
up surveillance footage of the unsub "—who may still
be hunting Jernigan. Unless we can get to him first…"

"Points well taken," Landon had to admit and thought
about Raquelle. "We'll keep looking for Eddie—and the
unsub, who's likely in Pimentel's hip pocket and would
still be expected to deliver on his assignment, if it's still
active."

Katie smiled supportively. "Sounds good to me."

He contemplated one of Eddie's known hangouts—the
Cridder Club—where he could have been hiding out. It
was where they met as his CI to exchange intel and discuss the investigation.

*I'll check it out and invite Raquelle along to keep her
in the loop*, Landon thought as he left the conference room
and got on his cell phone.

"HEY." LANDON TRIED to keep his tone measured as
Raquelle answered via speaker phone. "Are you busy
right now?"

"Not really," she told him. "I'm in my car after paying
Eddie's ex-girlfriend a visit."

"Is that right?" He didn't realize they were friends.
But then, how would he know the ins and outs of his ex-
wife's life these days? Or who she hung out with, even if
wishing it had been him.

"Yes." She paused. "I wanted to know if Eddie may
have been hiding out there."

"How did it go?" Landon asked curiously, while on
the road as well.

"He wasn't at the condo." Raquelle sighed. "Penelope
said she hadn't seen him in a while."

"Sorry you weren't able to locate Eddie," Landon said, knowing how much she wanted to find him alive. He wanted that too. But with each day—hell, every hour—that this wasn't the case, the less likely it was that Eddie would still emerge on his own two feet.

"Me too," Raquelle lamented. "Eddie called Penelope last week, indicating he was in trouble and hoped to find his way out of it. Likely with your help," she speculated.

"I never heard from him—until he left me a voice-mail the day he went missing," Landon told her and thought wistfully, *Wish I could have made contact with him.* "Maybe he intended to ask me to protect him…but never got the chance," he said.

"Hmm…" She took a breath. "If Eddie's still alive, he might still have that chance—if you're willing to step in."

"I am, of course." Landon watched the road. *First things first—tracking Eddie down before it's too late*, he thought. "If we find Eddie, I'll do everything in my power to see to it that he's safe from harm. Whatever it takes…"

"Thank you," Raquelle said with sincerity.

"No thanks necessary. As my CI, it's part of the job to minimize risks, while maximizing returns. Eddie knew that I had his back—if given the opportunity to get him out, if and when his cover was blown." Landon stopped at a light. "In fact, the reason I'm calling was to tell you that I'm headed to the Cridder Club on Gelinten Road in Gadwall Heights. It's where I met with Eddie a few times. The bartender, Rex Shepherd, was his friend and some-one Eddie could have reached out to for help. I thought you might want to meet me there."

"Yes, I would." Her voice lifted an octave. "I went there

once with Eddie. I'm not too far from where the club is located. I'll wait for you in the parking lot."

"Okay," Landon said, just minutes away himself. He wasn't holding out too much hope that Eddie had shown up there. But any possibility needed to be checked out. Beyond that, being in the presence of his ex-wife was something Landon relished, even if it was under less than ideal circumstances for both of them.

RAQUELLE ANXIOUSLY AWAITED LANDON, while hoping he might achieve better results in the search for Eddie. She had to believe he was still alive—even as she feared the odds might be stacking up against that with no word from her little brother to that effect. But she thought it possible that this deafening silence might have been his way of attempting to shield her from the murky art world he had ensconced himself into. One that clearly Landon was also heavily invested in, albeit on the right side of the law.

She recalled that he had immersed himself in fighting against white-collar criminals during much of their marriage and had been good at it—helping to put away some deserving individuals. Now Landon was focused on art-related crimes, which Raquelle was sure he excelled at just as much. Hadn't his dedication to the job played a big role in their marriage disintegrating?

Her reverie was interrupted when she saw Landon's Chevy Tahoe pull into the lot beside her car. She got out when he did and felt comfort in knowing they were both on the same page, at least when it came to wanting to find Eddie alive—if he was still somewhere to be located.

Landon flashed her a quick look and said, "Thanks for coming."

"Thanks for asking me to," Raquelle countered, realizing that he was on duty and could have chosen to go it alone—but didn't.

He nodded. "Let's see if Eddie has been here—"

"All right."

They went inside the midsized club and saw that it was mostly empty in the before noon time. Raquelle had actually considered that they might see Eddie sitting at a table, drinking beer as she had with him there. But there was no sign of her brother. Could he be hiding in a back room?

It wasn't long before Landon spotted the man he was looking for and told Raquelle, "There he is..."

She turned to the bar a few feet away, where the bartender was a tall and thickly built Native American man in his thirties with long brown hair across his shoulders, brown eyes, and a horseshoe mustache.

They walked over to him, and Landon asked knowingly, "Rex Shepherd, right?"

He stopped drying glasses, peering at them warily. "Yeah. Who are you?"

Lifting up his identification, Landon answered, "FBI Special Agent Briscoe—and this is Raquelle Jernigan, Eddie's sister..." That immediately commanded the man's attention.

Raquelle took this moment to speak up herself. "Eddie's been missing since his boat blew up the other day— and it was destroyed deliberately. As someone Eddie described as a good friend—" she chose to exaggerate this for all the right reasons "—we were wondering if he might have come to you for help?"

Rex scratched his mustache and said, "Yeah, Eddie came here—said some really bad people were after him.

He asked if he could borrow some money. I gave him what I had, which wasn't much but probably enough to catch a bus out of town."

"And when was this?" Landon asked intently, leaning against the bar counter.

"The day his boat exploded." Rex lowered his chin. "Said that after escaping the explosion, he had nowhere to turn…"

Landon frowned. "He did—but Eddie chose not to seek help."

Raquelle made a sound in agreement, feeling she would have done whatever she could have to help him. Landon clearly was of the same mind. Yet to Eddie, none of the options were to his liking. At least where it concerned involving her—which she had to respect.

Now they were left wondering if he had managed to get out of the area…the state maybe. Or had Eddie been prevented from doing this?

Just then, Landon's cell phone rang. He removed it from the pocket of his chinos, glanced at the caller ID, then answered workwise, "Briscoe…"

Raquelle watched as his expression went from nonchalant to distressed to something resembling resignation before Landon told the caller he was on his way.

"What is it?" Raquelle had to ask him, piqued, as he put the phone away.

"An adult male's body was discovered in the woods, not far from Eddie's apartment complex." Landon's brows knitted. "They think it could be Eddie…"

She choked up in hearing this but said, hoping against hope, "Maybe it's not him."

Landon placed a firm hand on her shoulder sympathetically. "I need to head over there. If you'd like, I can make the identification, if necessary, sparing you from—"

Raquelle cut in adamantly, "I don't need to be spared, Landon. If it is my brother, I need to see for myself—and deal with it…" No matter how painful it would be to her.

"Okay," he concurred. "You can follow me."

Chapter Eight

The last thing Landon wanted was for Raquelle to have to identify a corpse as the body of her brother. But who was he to tell her she didn't have that right? Especially when she had every right to face her greatest fears, one way or the other.

Similarly, Landon would not have wanted anyone but himself to make a positive identification had it been Raquelle who was found shot to death in the woods. In spite of the fact that her loss in that way—even though they were no longer married—would have been unimaginable.

When they arrived at the location off Qray Lane, which was about a quarter of a mile from Eddie's apartment complex, Landon flashed his ID to a slender twentysomething, curly blond-haired police officer, allowing him and Raquelle past the wooded area that had been cordoned off with yellow crime scene police tape.

As they approached the body, Landon grabbed Raquelle's shoulder, stopping her in her tracks in wanting to spare her from the potentially devastating news. "Are you sure you want to do this?" he asked in earnest.

She sucked in a deep breath, locked onto his eyes stably, and responded without blinking, "I'm sure. I owe that much to Eddie…if it's him…"

"Okay." Landon admired her courage as much as her strength in character that helped him fall in love with her when he did back in the day.

They were met by Homicide Detective Spencer Davidson of the Gadwall Heights Police Department. African American and in his forties, he was taller than Landon and just as well-built, with a shaved fade haircut, full goatee, and solid brown eyes.

After Landon introduced himself and Raquelle, Spencer, holding a pair of latex gloves, said bleakly, "Looks like the victim—who was discovered by our K-9 unit— may have been ambushed by someone. He was shot multiple times at pointblank range."

Landon furrowed his brow, while thinking ill at ease, *Time for the rubber to hit the road in seeing what— or who—we're looking at.* He gazed at Raquelle, who appeared to still herself in preparation at what they might see.

As Spencer stepped aside, they moved closer to the deceased. He was lying in a pool of blood on his back, wearing a blue half-zip pullover, jeans, and brown-white sneakers. Landon judged the man—with bullet wounds to the head and chest—who was tall and lanky, to be in his early to mid-thirties. He had dark hair in a short mullet and a square-shaped face with a skin tone and features that resembled those of Eddie Jernigan.

"It's not him," Raquelle asserted.

"No?" Landon asked to be sure for the record, though he concurred.

"No—this isn't my brother, Eddie," she reiterated with a heavy sigh.

"I'm in agreement with you there," he told her, while wondering if the close resemblance was happenstance or if the killer mistakenly believed the victim to be Eddie.

Without warning, Raquelle wrapped her arms around him in an emotional moment of relief, and Landon held her in his arms, happy to take one victory at a time as the search for Eddie continued.

"Thank goodness it wasn't him," she uttered softly.

Landon pulled away from her, peering into her watery eyes, as he said somberly, "Go home, Raquelle. This is still a murder investigation that needs to unwind. If anything comes up that warrants notification, I'll let you know."

"Okay." She nodded, then glanced at the decedent and back to him, before walking off.

After she left, Landon eyed the spent shell casings near the body, then asked Spencer, "Think this was a targeted hit?"

"Looks that way—be it a robbery, resistance, case of mistaken identity, wrong place, wrong time—who knows?"

"Yeah, except the shooter—for now," Landon surmised. "Any ID on the victim?"

"None that I could find," the detective said. "Could be the victim was homeless. We have more than our fair share of people living in the woods—or wherever they can lay their heads."

"Maybe." Landon creased his brow musingly. "We'll learn more about the dead man and the circumstances of death once the autopsy and crime scene investigation are completed."

"Exactly," Spencer concurred.

Landon left the wooded area while thinking about Eddie, who might have again cheated death if the victim was meant to be him. If not, the deceased was shot in cold blood by an unknown assailant and deserved justice.

Either way you slice it, Eddie may still be alive out there, trying to avoid a similar fate, he told himself as he got into his SUV. With Raquelle being forced to play a waiting game that neither of them wanted to lose.

At HOME THAT EVENING, Raquelle counted her blessings that Eddie hadn't been the person shot to death in the wooded area near his apartment. It was a close call, but the poor victim was someone else who ran into harm's way, for one reason or another. But he too must have had family that would now be left grieving his death and needing answers.

At least I still have hope that Eddie can get through his ordeal, Raquelle told herself, sitting on the piano bench, fingers on the keys. As she started to play the piano, she couldn't help but think about losing herself for a moment when embracing Landon in the woods. The sheer sense of relief that Eddie had not been shot to death brought her back to a comfort level she once felt with her ex-husband.

Till reality came crashing down like a tidal wave.

Or was it more of a reckoning that there might have still been something there between them?

Raquelle's thoughts were interrupted when her cell phone rang. She removed it from a pocket of her one-button ivory blazer and saw that the caller was Landon.

"Hey," he said tonelessly.

"Hey." She waited to hear if there was new info regarding Eddie. Perhaps another body had shown up in the woods?

"Eddie's still unaccounted for," Landon announced. "That's a good sign that he may still be out there somewhere—alive."

"I hope so." Raquelle looked at the piano. "But where?" *And if alive, how long can he last if he's still being hunted— and presumably running out of money?* she asked herself.

"I've been pondering that very question." Landon took a breath. "Is there any way possible that Eddie could have found his way to the Catawba tribal lands as a place to hide out?"

"Hmm…" She had to chew on that thought. They were both certainly proud members of the Catawba Nation, where their father was once on the executive committee. But she and Eddie had not been as active within the Catawba community as they probably should have been. Yet they both still kept in touch with some of those living on the reservation, leaving open the door that Eddie could have turned to them for refuge while being hunted. *Even if it meant keeping me out of the loop*, Raquelle told herself. "Yes, it's possible," she said, warming up to the idea in spite of Rock Hill, where the reservation was located, being more than an hour away by car.

"I think we should drive up to the reservation and see if Eddie is hiding there," Landon suggested. "If so, we can make sure he stays safe somewhere else, without endangering anyone on tribal lands."

"Okay," she said, not needing to pause for thought. The goal was to find Eddie before a killer did—if her brother truly was still among the living and in hiding. Only then could she feel that he was in safe hands, more or less. If this meant having to spend more time with her ex-husband in close proximity, then so be it. "When did you want to go?"

Landon answered, "I was thinking this afternoon—if that works for you. I can pick you up, and we can get there and back in a few hours—and see how it all plays out."

"I can make it work," she asserted. "I'll be ready when you arrive."

"All right. See you in a little while."

After she disconnected, Raquelle prepared herself for the excursion. She wondered if she should invite Landon inside for the first time since their divorce became official. Or would it seem too weird for either of them? As it was, she still felt the house belonged to both of them, despite her gaining complete ownership of it.

When she peeked through the window as Landon's duty vehicle pulled up to the house, Raquelle couldn't help but feel a combination of anxiety and excitement in taking this trip with him—while knowing that the very fate of Eddie could well be hanging in the balance.

LANDON WAITED IN his SUV for Raquelle to come out of the house that he once called home, admiring it and the surrounding property. He thought he might have seen her glancing out the window when he drove up but didn't take that as a sign that she was comfortable enough for him to encroach upon her personal space now that they had gone their separate ways. *I won't put pressure on her right now to let me in, figuratively and literally, till I feel she's ready*, he told himself.

After Raquelle came out of the house and climbed into the passenger seat, Landon gave her a brief smile, while captivated by her beauty, and said, "All set?"

"Yes," she replied coolly, putting on her seat belt. "Let's go see if Eddie is hiding on the rez."

As they drove down Interstate 77 North for the roughly seventy-five-mile drive, Landon considered the FBI, working in conjunction with the Bureau of Indian Affairs Missing and Murdered Unit, in prioritizing investigations of Indigenous persons who were missing, deceased, or otherwise unaccounted for. Eddie certainly fell under that premise, though Landon was focused more on the missing aspect of his CI at the moment rather than dead. It seemed reasonable that Raquelle's brother might have sought refuge in a safe space and comfort zone. The reservation would seem to fit the bill. And bring Raquelle back to a place she also once called home and filled a special place in her heart.

Landon turned to her musingly and couldn't help but ask what had been weighing on his mind ever since first seeing Raquelle again at the marina, "So, are you seeing anyone these days?"

She cast her eyes at him, thoughtful. "No," she replied, adding added, "No one special."

"I see." Landon liked the first answer better, even if he had no right to expect that she would have been saving herself for him over the last few years. He wondered if the second answer meant that she had been dating men who weren't special enough to hold her attention or desire for the long term.

"What about you?" Raquelle cut into his reverie.

"I'm also single right now," he told her honestly. "Between work and more work, my dating life has pretty much taken a hit since things ended between us."

"Hmm..." she cadenced, as if believing he was simply giving her a line.

"What?" He took his eyes off the road briefly to gaze at her profile. "You don't believe me?"

"Should I?" Raquelle flashed him a deadpan look. "Rumor has it that you've been keeping pretty busy with single-life escapades."

"Rumors, huh?" Landon laughed. "Don't believe everything you hear—or heard, Raquelle. Trust me when I say that you've been a hard act to follow." Even if he had tried to put himself out there when it seemed as though there was no going back for them.

She blushed. "Oh, really?"

"Yeah, really," he reiterated. "Romantic adventures can only go so far when they're empty of real feelings."

"Okay," she said, leaving it at that as they both sat silent for a few minutes.

During that time, Landon thought about the ups and downs of their marriage and how they ended up where they were. He couldn't really place a finger on how things deteriorated to the point of no return. Could she?

Finally, he turned toward her and asked straightforwardly, "What happened with us?"

Raquelle pursed her lips. "I think you know what happened. We let things come to a head and got divorced."

"That's the simple answer," he stated sharply, "but can you go into more specifics? I know we had conflicting work schedules and trouble communicating—I just need answers on how the marriage was allowed to fall apart without trying a hell of a lot harder to keep it going..."

She glared at him. "Are you saying it was all my fault?"

"No—nothing of the sort." Landon realized how it might have come across that way and needed to clarify. "I accept my fair share of the blame, believe me. We both let things slip away and have to own up to it."

Raquelle responded, "I have owned up to my role in the marriage failing. If you have too, then you know that we both spent way too much time being career obsessed— or so it seemed—which came at the expense of starting a family. I couldn't deal with that."

"I didn't think you were ready to have children at the time any more than I was," Landon spoke defensively, wishing he had been more secure with his job when the subject came up. "If I somehow misinterpreted that, you should have been more forthcoming in your point of view."

"Would it have made a difference?" she challenged him.

"Absolutely," he asserted. "What I wanted more than anything was to make you happy. That included having kids—something I always felt was in our future, but I only wanted to wait a little while longer while we gained a greater foothold in our careers and saved money. If you had wanted to get started sooner and expressed this, I would've done whatever I could to make that happen— including working fewer hours and cutting any corners necessary to make ends meet."

Raquelle seemed to allow this to sink in before she said contemplatively, "I guess I should've communicated better about this. I did want to wait a little longer to have a child but definitely was looking forward to that as soon as possible. I just wasn't sure we were on the same page there, which seemed to compound the trivial issues we had."

"We *were* on the same page," Landon tried his best to assure her, even if they were looking backward in what went wrong. "Though I didn't always express this, I wanted what you did in our personal lives—in spite of leaning too heavily on the minor grievances we threw at each other—and wish I'd fought harder to save the marriage." He eyed her, heartfelt in his sincerity. "And keep you in my life."

"We both could have—should have—done things differently, Landon," Raquelle told him, regret in her tone. "But we were younger, more immature, and less certain of who we were and what we wanted and needed in our lives." Her voice broke. "Like other failed marriages, hindsight gives us a clearer perspective—only too late to reverse course."

"Says who?" He tossed this question at her impulsively but meant it. "There's nothing out there that prevents divorced couples from giving it another go—only with greater clarity in what they want and what might be possible to achieve the second time around."

She gazed at him. "Do you really believe that?"

"Only if you do," he responded musingly. "No pressure. Just something to think about as two single— and lonely, at least in speaking for myself—exes who shouldn't close the door on the future that could be everything we ever wanted and then some." Landon waited a beat, then changed course for her sake. "But for now, I understand that finding Eddie—wherever he may be—is your top priority. I want that too," he assured her, even if he feared that the outcome could adversely affect any chance they had to give a relationship a second try—and whatever that could lead to.

They drove in silence the rest of the way before reaching Rock Hill in York County.

Chapter Nine

Raquelle was admittedly a bit apprehensive in the passenger seat as she thought about the conversation with Landon on their failed marriage and where it all went wrong. Had they thrown away a good thing for all the wrong reasons? Should they have worked much harder to communicate and tried to work their way through the issues that seemed to stymie them—most notably, the timing on when they should start a family?

Was there really any chance that in learning from their mistakes, they could rectify them? And possibly restart their relationship?

Or was Landon living in a fantasy land at the mere suggestion? Did he truly believe there could still be a happily-ever-after for them, in spite of having already gone their separate ways for years now?

Raquelle was lonely too, even if she chose not to focus on it much as it was often too depressing to digest. But Landon had thrown her a lifeline of sorts for a possible future together. Should she grab onto it? Or would this only lead to history repeating itself?

As they approached the Catawba Nation, Raquelle's thoughts turned to the prospect that Eddie had taken shelter there. Would he really hide out on the reservation from those who wanted him dead? Was this where her brother expected her to find him and offer support?

I have to believe Eddie's still alive, and though he could be anywhere, the rez is as good a place as anywhere he won't likely be found by outsiders, Raquelle told herself, glancing at Landon, deep in thought behind the wheel.

They drove down the Avenue of the Nations, passing by the farmers' market at the Catawba Nation's food-distribution center and the senior center. Then came the twenty-two-acre Black Snake Farm and walking trails before driving past the Catawba Cultural Center on Tom Steven Road.

"Seems like old times," Landon commented, breaking the quiet between them.

"It does in some ways," Raquelle acknowledged, even if it felt oddly strange in other ways as it related to them in current times. She had treasured visiting the reservation during the early part of their marriage, with Landon showing a keen interest in her heritage, which she sincerely appreciated. The Catawba Indians had resided on its ancestral lands for thousands of years alongside the Catawba River—while expanding its tribal citizenship across the country, even getting into the casino and gaming industries in the Carolinas.

Landon had readily welcomed learning about her heritage. This meant the world to Raquelle, the ending of their relationship notwithstanding. Just as she embraced his taking on Native American art crime as an FBI special agent in spite of the negative connotations regarding her brother. Eddie had chosen to sell counterfeit art and involve himself with the wrong people—and right people by becoming Landon's CI—and was now paying the price. The only way for him to own up to his mistakes was to have a chance for a fresh start.

Assuming he's still alive, Raquelle told herself, sweeping away a wayward hair that fell onto her forehead.

Landon asked, "So, where do we start in looking for your brother?"

"I'd say the home of his friend since childhood, Jay Locklear," she replied thoughtfully. "If Eddie were to come here at all, Jay would probably know about it—and where to find him—"

"All right, let's pay Locklear a visit."

Raquelle directed him to the address on Marta's Court where Jay, who worked for the Tribal Historic Preservation Office, lived in a two-story home with a well-manicured lawn and magnolias lining the property. A red Jeep Renegade sat in the driveway in front of a closed garage door.

The front door to the house opened and Jay stepped outside, locking it. In his early thirties, he was tall and of medium build, with a long brunette braid and a landing-strip goatee.

"Hi, Jay." Raquelle offered him a soft smile as he approached them.

He grinned at her and said, "Well, look who the wind blew in. Hey, Raquelle."

When he gazed at Landon, she introduced him. "This is FBI Special Agent Landon Briscoe—and my ex-husband," she added to make him less intimidating as a member of federal law enforcement.

Landon stuck out his hand in a friendly gesture. "Nice meeting you, Jay."

"You too," he replied, eyeing him warily. Jay turned back to Raquelle. "So, to what do I owe this pleasure…?"

She got right to the point. "We're looking for Eddie."

"Eddie?" Jay cocked a brow. "Is he in some kind of trouble?"

Landon answered bluntly, "More like trouble is out to kill him—if he's not already dead. Eddie was my confidential informant on a case I'm working on. Someone blew up his boat, apparently expecting Eddie to be on it. He managed to escape somehow and appears to be on the run." Landon exchanged glances with Raquelle, then looked at Jay. "We thought he might have sought refuge on the reservation…"

Raquelle added, with urgency, "If he's here, Jay, you need to tell us. Eddie's life could well depend on it. Not to mention others in the Catawba Indian Nation could also be at risk."

Jay favored her with a straight look and said flatly, "Sorry to hear about the boat and Eddie missing and in danger—but he's not here."

"Are you sure about that?" Landon pressed, peering at him.

"Yeah." Jay met his gaze. "Feel free to check the house if you want. No one's inside but my dog, Piper. He's a twelve-year-old golden Lab that's a bit ornery but otherwise harmless."

Raquelle wanted to take him up on checking out the house—if only to verify his truthfulness, though having no particular reason to disbelieve him—but Landon responded, "That won't be necessary."

Jay nodded. Folding his arms, he asked Raquelle, "What makes you think Eddie would have come to the reservation? Not exactly like he's been part of this community of late, any more than you've been."

Ouch, Raquelle thought, feeling the sting. "We've always been a part of the Catawba Nation. That will never change," she expressed. "No matter where we live or happen to be doing in our lives."

"Okay." Jay sighed. "You made your point."

"As for Eddie showing up on your doorstep," she told him, "it was just a thought since you're his longtime friend and someone he could trust to keep him out of harm's way."

"Believe me, I would do anything for Eddie, if I could," Jay insisted. "But I have no idea where he is. You could talk to Chief Quincy Marsh. But I'm sure he'd say the same thing. Not many places on the rez Eddie could go unseen."

"I'm sure you're right about that," she conceded.

Landon handed Jay his card. "If you happen to hear from Eddie, give me a call."

"I'll do that." Jay stuck the card into the back pocket of his light denim jeans. "I have to get to work. Nice seeing you again, Raquelle, even if under these circumstances."

"You too, Jay." She also wished it was a less stressful visit. Maybe that could come later, once Eddie was found, safe and sound.

After Jay had left in his Jeep, Landon asked Raquelle in the SUV, "What do you think?"

She twisted her lips, pondering this. "If Eddie's on the loose and not being held captive, he's probably still somewhere closer to home and familiar surroundings. Or else he's left the state altogether for his own safety." Both were preferable to her brother being already dead and buried.

"A statewide endangered person alert has been issued for Eddie and been extended to nearby states," Landon told her. "Though there have been no credible leads to his whereabouts thus far, that doesn't mean he's not still out there—maintaining a low profile till he's ready to make contact with one of us."

"Hope so," Raquelle said, even as she was finding it harder with each passing day to keep the faith that they hadn't already gotten to her brother—meaning she had seen him for the last time.

Landon put a hand on her shoulder and said evenly, "Let me take you home."

"All right." She fastened her seat belt, and both were thoughtful during much of the drive to Dryer Woods.

"Do you want to come inside?" Raquelle surprised Landon by asking as he pulled up to the house, inviting him in for the first time since the divorce became official. "Nothing's really changed much over the years—it was perfect the way it was—but you're welcome to check it out anyway if you'd like."

"I would like to," he answered without delay, relishing the chance to see again the house Landon once believed they would spend the rest of their lives in as a married couple.

She smiled. "Okay."

They left the car and went inside the house. It took him only a moment or two before Landon acclimated himself with the familiar surroundings as a flashback of the time they spent there together came flooding back to him like a tidal wave of mostly good memories. He noted some subtle changes in accent pieces and arrangement of furniture but otherwise felt as though he had stepped back in time.

"Looks great," he told her while gazing at the piano and wondering how often she put it to use these days.

Raquelle grinned. "You deserve as much credit for that as I do," she suggested.

Landon wasn't sure he agreed as, aside from choosing the house together, it was her natural inclination for interior decoration that made the place what it was. Apart from that, she deserved to be able to hang on to something that helped make their marriage so special. He smiled and said graciously, "I'm just glad you have somewhere to feel at home."

She considered this thoughtfully and asked, "Would you like something to drink—wine, coffee or…"

"Wine would be nice," he replied.

"All right."

Landon ventured further into the great room and walked up to the piano. He sat on the bench backward and admired the surroundings, wishing he was still a part of them. *I blew it*, he told himself for his part in acting prematurely in wanting out of their marriage. Maybe there was still hope yet to fix that mistake.

"Here you go," Raquelle said, handing him the goblet of red wine, having poured herself a glass as well.

He grinned. "Thanks." She sat beside him, and he asked, "So, do you play this much?"

"As often as time and the mood allows," she said.

"That's great. No talent like yours should ever go to waste."

"True, and thanks." Raquelle eyed him. "How about you—still playing your guitar?"

Landon sipped the wine. "Yeah, I do play it on occasion. But it was more fun when I got to jam with you..."

She blushed. "We did make a good team—musically speaking," she added, as if needing to clarify in differentiating that from their failed married life.

"I agree—the music was great." He felt the other good times during the marriage were even better but didn't want to cause a stir by going there and reminding her where they went wrong.

After she drank some wine, Raquelle looked at him with a frown and asked, "Is it unrealistic to think that Eddie could have somehow survived—after at least one attempt on his life that we know of—and hasn't been kidnapped and tortured, while being kept in a dungeon somewhere? Without reaching out to either of us since the boat explosion, it makes me believe he's not really waiting to make some grand entry, as if rising from the dead."

Landon could not fault her sense of logic. He recalled Eddie's voicemail to him:

"Landon...they want me dead. You have to help me... I need a way out of this—before I'm silenced forever..."

Had this been the case? Was he being held for info or leverage as a prelude to eliminating him from the face of the earth?

Were they just spinning their wheels trying to find him?

Even as Landon had his doubts too about Eddie's chances for survival, short of his corpse coming to light in an official homicide, there was no reason to extinguish Raquelle's hope of finding her brother alive. No matter that the odds were getting slimmer with each dead end.

Placing a hand on her lap, Landon gazed at Raquelle

and said convincingly, "It's not unrealistic to believe that your brother is still out there somewhere—alive and as well as could be expected while on the move. Just because he hasn't contacted us doesn't mean he's unable to due to death. There's no body as yet, even as the search continues. Or any credible evidence that a kidnapping occurred. Maybe there's a reason for that. Eddie may have chosen to lie low and silent while he assesses his problems and what he may see as his best interests in moving forward."

"You really think so?" Her eyes locked on his.

"Yeah, I do." Landon set his jaw. "So long as there's no sign of Eddie, let's not throw in the towel on finding him alive." *After recruiting Eddie as my CI, the least I can do is give her a reason to remain hopeful here*, he told himself, then tasted the wine.

"Okay," Raquelle assented and drank as well.

Landon glanced at the piano. "Will you play something for me?"

"If you'd like." She turned around on the bench, set the wineglass down, and put her fingers on the piano keys.

He watched as she played a traditional Native American piece with ease, bringing him back to the joy of her music that had been missing in his life.

In the moment, Landon couldn't help but think that Raquelle looked more gorgeous than ever. He suddenly felt—or maybe not so suddenly—an overwhelming desire to kiss her. Would she object, ruining the good vibes that seemed to be emerging again?

As he contemplated this, Raquelle stopped playing, tilted her face, gazed at him, and planted her lips on his mouth for a tentative kiss. She pulled away quickly and again searched his eyes before saying timidly, "I probably shouldn't have done that."

Wanting to seize the moment, Landon responded brusquely, "You've got no complaints from me. If the truth be told, kissing you was something I've wanted to do ever since walking in that door—if not before. So, if it's all the same to you, I'd like to try that again. Only longer this time..."

Raquelle nodded. "Yes, let's try it again."

He sat his wineglass on the piano, cupped her cheeks, and kissed her, tasting the wine from her lips, turning him on even more.

The kiss lasted a full five heated minutes, and Landon felt that they hadn't missed a beat in the art of kissing each other as if time had stood still. He was aroused enough to want to take this to another level and make love to Raquelle. Yet he refrained from even attempting to go down that road, not wanting to overstep his bounds. Or misread a kiss for something more.

I can't let a good thing slip away again by moving too fast, too soon, Landon thought. He pried their lips apart and said sweetly, "That was nice."

Raquelle touched her lips blushingly. "Yes, it was."

Glad you thought so, he mused. "I should probably go." If this were to happen, he didn't want her to feel rushed or in any way uncertain about what she wanted from him.

She nodded, thoughtful. "All right."

After being walked to the door, Landon turned to his ex-wife and said, "Thanks for inviting me in."

Raquelle grinned. "I'm glad I did—and that we got a chance to talk."

"Me too." *And kiss*, he thought. He smiled at her. "See you later."

"Bye, Landon."

He left, hoping this was the start of a new beginning for them. Or was it only a short trip down memory lane that had no real future?

Or was it contingent on whether or not Eddie was still alive and able to be a part of their lives, looking ahead?

Chapter Ten

On Monday morning, Landon stood in the conference room before other members of the Art Crime Team, going over the latest news on their current investigation. That included Eddie's still unknown status and the homicide near his apartment complex.

With the stylus pen in hand, Landon put a close-up image of a dead man's face on the big screen. "Two days ago, this person was found shot to death in a wooded area by Qray Lane in Gadwall Heights—just a short distance from the Bechum Apartments complex on Klatton Road, where Eddie Jernigan lives." Landon did his best to keep his former brother-in-law's status in the present tense, wanting it to be that way. "The victim was identified as thirty-four-year-old Lim Ramírez. Described by the Gadwall Heights PD as a drifter. According to the Falona County Coroner's Office, Ramírez was shot three times—twice to the head and once in the chest—at close proximity, causing significant blood loss. A shot to the back of the head was described as the fatal injury. The manner of death, not too surprisingly, was ruled a homicide. Ballistics determined that the bullets and spent shell casings recovered were fired from the gun barrel of a Korth 2.75-inch Carry Special .357 Magnum hand-gun with five lands and grooves and a right-hand twist."

Landon created a split screen, keeping the macabre image of Ramírez on one side and putting a photograph of Eddie beside it. "I have reason to believe that my CI, Eddie Jernigan, may have been the intended victim—corresponding with the IED used to blow up his boat and the proximity to Jernigan's apartment."

He switched to a still shot of a tall, white male, wearing a hooded sweatshirt—the hood over his head—jeans and dark sneakers. "This was taken from a surveillance cam-era in the vicinity of the wooded area where Ramírez's body was discovered," Landon said before putting up two other still shots side by side. "The unsub resembles a suspect seen running from the marina just before Ed-die's boat exploded as well as a man who was captured on a campus security video lurking around a parking lot at Braedon College in Joyllis Hills. He fit the description of an unsub seen checking out the vehicle of Eddie's sister, Raquelle Jernigan, a theater professor—who happens to be my ex-wife." Waiting a beat as that settled in, Landon finished with, "So, to make a long story short, there's a good chance that the bomber of Eddie's pontoon also shot to death Lim Ramírez."

"And where does this leave Eddie?" Katie questioned, an edge to her voice, while standing. "I know he's still missing—but is he even alive at this point? Maybe Ramírez's killer got to your CI first..."

Landon regarded her and responded musingly, "That's always a possibility. Just as it is that Eddie was taken against his will and out of sight. But the fact that Eddie apparently drove his own car away from the marina—and abandoned the vehicle soon after he'd borrowed money from a bartender at the Cridder Club on Gelinten Road in Gadwall Heights—suggests that he may still be alive and trying to stay that way. Though there's been no activity with his credit cards, which could be deliberate so as to avoid law enforcement as well right now, the fact that we have nothing to indicate an abduction or homicide where it concerns my CHS tells me that Eddie is more likely than not to be among the living than dead."

"Makes sense, all things considered," Zach uttered from his chair. "Honestly, I hope your CI is still around to help us put the screws to Ivan Pimentel and his criminal operation."

"You and me both," Landon told him forthrightly. "Until such time, we'll continue to piece together our Native American art-theft-and-forgery case against Pimentel and his cronies."

THAT AFTERNOON, KATIE MET with her boyfriend, Tony Razo, the District of South Carolina's US marshal, for lunch at Rundle's Deli on Main Street in downtown Columbia.

Tony, thirty-five, was six feet tall—a few inches taller than her—well-built, and handsome with blue eyes, jet-black hair in a low fade undercut and short sideburns. Like her, he'd never been married but wasn't opposed to marrying, if it felt right. She was of the same mind and more than willing to take it one day at a time—after dating for ten months now—and making a concerted effort to be together as much as possible, given their often-conflicting work schedules.

Katie listened with interest as Tony droned on about

the latest assignments to fall into his jurisdiction while she nibbled on a veggie sub and he had a chicken-salad sub. They split a side dish of ranch fries.

After rattling off the first three names on the US Marshals Service's Fifteen Most Wanted fugitives list, Tony practically bragged, "Last night, we tracked down in Charleston a man wanted on a number of federal child-sexual-exploitation charges. Getting him off the streets was a top priority to protect children."

"I'm glad to hear that," Katie told him, hating the thought of any children being sexually exploited for the profits of child victimizers.

Tony grabbed a ranch fry and said equably, "It's what we do." He smiled and said, "More good news... I heard that one of our tactical K-9s, Alfie, who was shot multiple times last week during a raid of a house in Florence, was released from the hospital this morning. He's expected to make a complete recovery and get back to work for us."

"Amazing, and thank goodness for Alfie's courage under fire," she marveled.

"Yeah," he concurred.

When the conversation switched to her latest cases, Katie mentioned several that she was juggling as part of the Bureau's Art Crime Team—including the Native American art-theft-and-forgery investigation, and her impending testimony in court following the recent arrest of a couple for interstate transportation of stolen modern art prints.

Tony grinned. "Impressive."

She raised a brow. "You think?"

"Of course—especially where it concerns you." He tilted his face and planted a kiss on her mouth.

"Good answer." Katie showed her teeth and dug into the veggie sub. She had just begun to elaborate on the Native American art-crimes case and the disappearance of Eddie Jernigan when she spotted Landon and Zach entering the deli.

Tony invited them over to the table, having gotten to know the special agents in the course of their professional intersection on investigations. Katie had no problem with the company of her colleagues, whom she considered like family. Or at least was comfortable with them in pretty much any setting—including a restaurant.

Landon and Zach sat around the table as Tony joked, "Don't you FBI agents have anything better to do than stalk my girlfriend?"

Landon, whose tray had a ham-and-cheese sandwich and coffee on it, chuckled and said, "Katie would never let us get away with it, even if we had no better way to spend our time."

Zach, a club sandwich and glass of lemonade on his tray, quipped, "Well, we did pose as a couple recently— but don't tell my wife, Celeste—so you'll have to forgive me if I find myself wanting to stay close to Katie."

"Enough already, you guys." She laughed, embarrassed with the attention. "Keep me out of this, please!"

"Done!" Landon said. "You've been removed from the stalking files."

She blushed. "Thanks."

Tony kissed her cheek. "Now that that's over and done with, let's talk about your latest case and where things stand with the missing CHS…"

Landon bit into his sandwich and said thoughtfully, "He's out there somewhere. Not sure if Eddie's dead or alive—but my money's on the latter at this point. Just a gut feeling. The key is to track him down before reputed art-crime boss Ivan Pimentel can take him out."

Zach sipped lemonade and said frankly, "We're definitely up against the clock here in both locating Jernigan to bolster our case against Pimentel and holding the art dealer accountable for a growing list of crimes. The two aren't necessarily mutually exclusive, but obviously the CI's testimony—and any evidence he may still have collected—would go a long way toward sealing the deal in a Pimentel conviction."

Katie sipped tea and argued, "The case can be made with or without Eddie Jernigan's input. Obviously, though, whoever blew up his boat believed that silencing him—through kidnapping or killing—could only help matters when it came to preventing Eddie from telling what he knew as a CI."

"If and when you find him," Tony said, wiping his mouth with a napkin, "you can always put Jernigan in the Witness Security Program to keep him out of harm's way till he can deliver on his intel."

"Yeah, that is an option." Landon nodded. "We'll see how it goes."

Katie gazed at him. She also saw WITSEC as a possibility, should Eddie manage to have survived his ordeal. But how would Landon's ex-wife feel about being out of touch with her brother—perhaps for a while?

"Eddie's disappearance and the not knowing has to be hard on your ex." Katie peered at Landon. She'd never met Raquelle Jernigan but had picked up through conversation how much he still cared for her.

"It has been," Landon acknowledged, leaning back in

his chair, brooding. "Raquelle's strong, though. Whatever happens, she'll get through it."

"Maybe with your help," Katie said, "based on my women's intuition."

He grinned. "Maybe."

"Something going on between you and your ex that we should know about, Briscoe?" Zach asked teasingly as he grabbed one of their ranch fries off the plate.

Landon squared his chin. "Yeah, something," he confessed. "Just not quite sure what it is at this stage."

"Well, when you find out, be sure to let us know."

"I will," he said thoughtfully.

Katie smiled at him, imagining what it would be like to marry for the first time as she eyed Tony. Much less go for a repeat—unlike with Zach, who preferred to try again with someone else. In Landon's case, perhaps the one who got away was the woman he was truly meant to be with.

RAQUELLE SAT ON an ergonomic desk chair in her small but neatly organized office in Blakemoor Hall on Pattery Lane. Seated on the other side of the electric adjustable desk was Vera Mahaffey, her GTA, who was grading papers, while Raquelle was busy preparing an assignment for her class. As she did so, her thoughts slipped back to Saturday when she'd kissed Landon. It was hardly a planned action on her part, but it was one that Raquelle relished. Kissing her ex-husband somehow felt right. He seemed to be of the same mind. And body, given both their bodies seemed to tense up while reacquainting themselves with this rather intimate act.

"So, how was your weekend?" Vera asked, as if only to start a conversation.

"Good." Once again, that sweet kiss entered Raquelle's head. "How about yours?"

"Same." Vera then spoke glowingly about her new girlfriend.

"Nice." Raquelle smiled and looked at her laptop. Her mind went to Eddie. She wondered if he would ever reach out to her—if he was able to. Or if there was any way to communicate with him without compromising his safety. Or hers. "Have you seen anyone else—or the same person—hanging around my car?" she asked Vera.

The GTA shook her head. "Not that I can recall."

"Good." *At least where it concerns me being a possible target of the man who may have blown up Eddie's boat*, Raquelle told herself. Or some stalker, knowing that there had been several reports of stalking on campus recently. But if Eddie chose to show up at the college for help, she would welcome this.

"Maybe it was nothing," Vera said, running fingers through her hair.

"Maybe." Raquelle wasn't sure she believed that. Nor did Landon seem to think that it was necessarily unrelated to his investigation. Or Eddie's disappearance.

After she left the office, Raquelle got a call from Landon as she stepped outside for some fresh air.

"Hey," he said in a spirited tone of voice.

"Hey." She put the phone closer to her ear.

"I was wondering if you'd like to have dinner with me tonight—if you didn't have any other plans."

"No other plans," Raquelle freely admitted. "What restaurant?"

"Actually, I'll be making the meal," Landon told her.

"It will give you a chance to check out my place, assuming that's okay with you?"

"Yes, I'd like that." She had been curious about his condominium since he moved to Columbia. "What time?"

"How does six thirty sound?"

"Perfect."

"Good," he said. "I'll text you the address."

Raquelle smiled. "All right."

After disconnecting, she headed back to her office before an afternoon class, looking forward to spending more time with her ex.

HE FOLLOWED RAQUELLE JERNIGAN as she left the college in her Infiniti Q50. Keeping a safe distance, he wondered what she knew about her brother's activities. Not to mention his whereabouts.

It irked him to think that he'd shot and killed the wrong man instead of his intended target, Eddie Jernigan. The fact that Jernigan had somehow managed to escape death more than once led him to believe that the art dealer's luck would run out shortly.

And not a moment too soon.

His employer, Ivan Pimentel—and sidekick, Yusef Abercrombie—were none too happy that he hadn't held up his end of the bargain in ridding Pimentel of a big problem. He'd made it perfectly clear that Jernigan being alive was not an option.

Meaning his own life was on the line as long as Eddie continued to breathe.

But was the snitch actually breathing these days? Had Eddie been blown up in the boat, only to be buried in the lake? It made sense, as this had been the plan all along and should've gone without a hitch.

The fact that Eddie had apparently not been seen since was a good sign. But still not the concrete proof he needed that the man was dead.

He had trailed Eddie's sister to the Catawba Nation reservation, where she undoubtedly went looking for Jernigan—alongside the FBI special agent, Landon Briscoe, her ex-husband, whom Eddie was feeding information.

The two had come away empty-handed. Which told him that Jernigan was nowhere to be found. Maybe that was a good thing. Being unreachable meant that he was keeping his big mouth shut, one way or the other. Assuming he was still around to cause trouble.

He watched as Raquelle Jernigan turned onto Velick Road toward her house. Keeping his distance, he saw her pull into her driveway.

Could she be hiding her brother at the house, in spite of the visit to the reservation?

There was no clear indication of this when he'd surveilled the residence earlier. But what if this were the case?

Then he would need to do what he had to do in his own best interests.

If push came to shove, he might have to take the next big step of planting a bomb inside the house to blow it to bits.

Even if that meant Raquelle blew up with it. And Eddie, if he was holed up there.

He drove past the house nonchalantly, already making contingency plans to take things to the next level—while keeping Ivan Pimentel and Yusef Abercrombie at bay.

Chapter Eleven

Raquelle had to admit that she was a little giddy, like a teenager on a first date, going to Landon's condo for dinner. It had been years since they ate a dinnertime meal together. But the time apart and reflection—along with them having a common purpose in finding Eddie—had softened the strained nature of their relationship. She had no idea if their chemistry and kissing meant there was more to come or if it was just a mutual pause in the status quo for old times' sake.

After driving into the underground parking garage, Raquelle parked in a guest spot and headed for the elevator. With her hair down, she wore a rose-colored midi shirtdress and brown slingback sandals. *Hope I'm not over- or underdressed*, she thought when riding up to the condo.

When Landon opened the door, he beamed at her. "Hey."

"Hey." Raquelle smiled back. "I might be a little early."

He countered, "In fact, you're right on time. The food's ready. Come in."

"Thank you." She stepped inside the condo, her nostrils immediately picking up the appealing scent of dinner.

Landon closed the door and said, giving her a once-over, "You look great."

"Thanks, again." Raquelle blushed. She took him in, noting that he was freshly shaven and wearing a lilac-colored herringbone shirt, dark blue pants, and black loafers. "You clean up nicely yourself," she had to say truthfully.

"I try my best when a good opportunity to get out of work attire presents itself." He flashed his teeth. "So, this is it—the place I've been renting for half a year now."

Raquelle scanned the condo's layout and furnishings before stating, "It's wonderful, Landon. Suits you, actually."

"You think?"

"Yes, for a single man on the go." *Did I really just give a stamp of approval for my ex-husband's bachelor life as a divorcé?* Raquelle asked herself. "It's just a nice, charming condo," she tried to correct.

"Glad you approve." Landon laughed. "I was lucky to land it. That being said, it doesn't really compare to the house we bought and its charms. I'm happy that you agreed to keep it and watch the value grow over time."

"Thanks to you," Raquelle said, giving credit to where it was due. Even if she felt a little guilty in getting the better of the deal in their divorce settlement.

Landon told her, "In all fairness, it was the least I could do to try and end things between us on a good note and make sure you were left with something wholly deserving."

She colored, feeling almost speechless in his selflessness at a time when the legality of their romance had come to a crashing halt. "I appreciate it," she managed to say before zeroing in on the familiar acoustic guitar on a wooden guitar stand. "I see you're still playing the guitar."

"Yeah, a bit." Landon gazed at it. "I'm afraid that more often than not it just collects dust these days. My bad."

"I agree—as you're a good guitarist," she stressed.

"Thanks," he said. "But I'd take your piano playing over my guitar any day of the week, if I could."

"Hmm..." She met his eyes thoughtfully. "Maybe we'll get to play together again one of these days."

"I would definitely be on board with that." He grinned. "Well, feel free to freshen up—there's a half bath just off the kitchen—and I'll serve dinner."

"Smells wonderful."

"Hope you like it just as much."

After washing her hands, Raquelle joined Landon in the kitchen. "What can I do to help?"

"Anything you want," he said half-jokingly. "Plates are in there—" he pointed at the two-toned upper cabinets "—and glasses in that one. Silverware's already out."

She smiled. "Setting the table coming right up."

He nodded. "As for the meal itself, I decided to go with braised chicken thighs, pasta salad, dinner rolls, and white wine to wash it down."

"Spoken like a true chef," Raquelle said with a chuckle. "Who would've thought?" Since she'd done much of the cooking during their marriage, this was a new and exciting side to him that she would need to get used to.

"Not me." Landon laughed. "I'm not quite ready to give up my day job just yet, but I've gotten used to having to cook for myself every now and then—when not taking the easy way out."

"Since when have you ever taken the easy way out of anything?" she challenged him, knowing that he rarely did anything without giving thought to it beforehand. For better or worse.

"Good point." He chuckled and grabbed the plate with the chicken thighs. "Let's go eat."

They sat on rustic reclaimed curved-back cowhide chairs at the barnwood pedestal dining table.

Raquelle proclaimed, "Mmm, this is delicious!"

Landon laughed. "Glad you're enjoying the food. I'm still kind of a work in progress as a chef but will happily take the compliment."

"You should," she told him, shamelessly forking more pasta salad. "It's really good."

"Thanks." He sliced his knife into a chicken thigh. "Yeah, it's tasty—but I'm enjoying the company even more, to be honest about it."

"Is that so?" she asked, fluttering her lashes.

"Yes," he told her flatly. "It's nice having you around again."

"I feel the same," she admitted, even if unsure what it meant in the evolution of their involvement with one another.

Landon grinned, sipping wine. "Good."

They were more than halfway through with the meal when Raquelle asked curiously, "What will happen to your case if Eddie isn't able to fulfill his part of the bargain as your CI?"

"We have more than enough to get a conviction of the main players in our investigation of Native American art forgery and theft," Landon told her. "When we have all our ducks lined up, we'll push forward." He angled his face. "Eddie still remains an integral part of the case," he stressed. "He can fill in some blanks that only someone with real inside intel can accomplish."

Raquelle gazed across the table contemplatively. "Assuming they haven't already finished off my brother..." *I hate to go there with such a relaxing meal, but ignoring the real possibilities won't make them disappear,* she told herself, biting into a dinner roll.

"It's an assumption I'm not ready to make—and neither should you," Landon argued. "We'll continue to search for Eddie with the belief that until his body shows up, he's still with us—"

She nodded, grateful for his support and hopefulness that her brother was alive and well. "Thank you."

"There is one thing you might need to consider," he told her, a break in his voice. "If we do find Eddie and he's able to testify, he may need to go into the Witness Security Program for his own safety."

Raquelle flinched, having gotten some basic knowledge on the federal WITSEC as the former wife of an FBI special agent. The idea of finding Eddie only to lose him again as her only living relative was heartbreaking. But needing to look over his shoulder twenty-four seven would be even worse for him—and her.

"I understand," she said, tasting her wine. "Convincing Eddie may not be so easy. But I'm sure he would prefer to set up shop elsewhere and live a normal life, rather than continually put himself at risk."

"I think so too," Landon told her, lifting his own wineglass. "Anyway, I just wanted to throw that out there as something to consider down the line."

"I'll do that," Raquelle promised while knowing that

they weren't quite at the point for looking too far ahead on this front. Not with Eddie still missing—his whereabouts unknown. But where it concerned their own relationship, she was beginning to believe that looking ahead wasn't a bad thing. Especially when she could see herself being with Landon again. Or was that not where things were headed?

"Now it's my turn to ask you to play music—on your guitar," Raquelle said after they had cleared the table.

Landon smiled. "Okay, sure."

They walked over to the guitar, and he grabbed it, wondering if this would be a good time to serenade her with a song like the old days. Maybe not just yet. He wasn't quite ready to push the envelope, preferring that she took the lead for what might happen.

Landon started playing the guitar, keeping the rock song lighthearted and fun. Raquelle laughed, clearly enjoying it.

"That was nice," she told him when he finished.

It will be nicer when we can combine my guitar and your piano playing in perfect harmony, he thought, but he said smoothly, "Thanks."

Raquelle eyed him and asked boldly, "So, do you want to show me where you sleep?"

"I'd be happy to." Landon kept his voice on an even keel, though his heart skipped a beat at the suggestion. "This way."

He led her down a short hall to the primary bedroom that had its own en suite and watched as she scanned the spacious room with its farmhouse furnishings and large windows. Her gaze fell on the rustic king bed and its dark orange duvet cover.

"Nice," Raquelle marveled.

Not half as nice as it was sharing a primary suite with you what seems like ages ago but is still very fresh in my memories, Landon told himself. He responded, "Thanks. It gets the job done for the intended purpose."

She eyed him desirously. "Think it can do the same for unintended—or impulsive—purposes…?"

"Oh, I'm sure of it," he assured her without hesitation.

"Hmm… Let's see about that…" Raquelle lifted her chin and waited for him to kiss her lips. "Go for it!"

Landon grinned. He was more than happy to oblige as he took her cheeks in his hands and brought their mouths together in a stirring, passionate kiss. *It's such a turn-on kissing you*, he thought, fully aware of the contours of their bodies pressed close together.

She pulled back and, gazing into his eyes, asked, "Is going down this road really a good idea?"

He held the gaze and answered, "Yes—one that I'd say has been years in the making. I want you, Raquelle."

"I want you too," she stressed, pausing. "I'm not on the pill."

"I have protection," he told her, recognizing that no matter their mutual desire and wish to have children someday, both were responsible enough to make sure it was when they were ready. To Landon, the notion of that happening in happy matrimony would be even better, should this ever morph in that direction again.

"Good," Raquelle said enthusiastically.

He opened the wooden nightstand drawer and removed the condom packet, tossing it onto the bed. "Ready to go."

She smiled yearningly. "Make love to me, Landon."

"With pleasure." He beamed and began removing his clothes as fast as he could while watching her do the same. Taking in Raquelle's body, Landon saw that it was as perfect as he remembered—with small but firm breasts, a lean stomach, long, shapely legs, and delicate feet and toes.

Likewise, he saw her checking him out too and was unabashed in giving her approval. "I see you're still in great shape," she uttered.

"So are you," he said candidly. "More than that, you're gorgeous, Raquelle."

"Umm…" She blushed. "Prove it."

Feeling the surge of desire rise in him like the tide, Landon scooped her up into his arms and carried her over to the bed while they kissed fervently, as though waiting even a moment longer had become unbearable.

RAQUELLE COULD BARELY contain her craving to be with her ex-husband, though she would not have thought this would even be possible before very recently. But the sparks between them had clearly never been fully extinguished, and now she only wanted to see them reignited for the moment at hand. Without much deep thought into any long-term implications—or complications.

When Landon started kissing her from head to toe and in between, while making good use of his hands in simultaneous and adroit stimulation, Raquelle felt instant and powerful gratification. "Mmm, that feels so wonderful," she cooed with the climax.

"You deserve this," he told her, seemingly determined

to satisfy her. And had, as the sensations of intimate pleasure coursed throughout Raquelle's body.

"So do you." As much as she enjoyed being the center of *his* attention, Raquelle wasn't so selfish that she didn't want him to experience the same gratification, while aware that he had held back his own sexual release. Turning the tables, she used her own kisses and fingers for some quid pro quo and felt Landon's body tense. "I want you," she uttered desperately.

"I need you," he replied urgently as their bodies lined up side by side.

"Take me," Raquelle demanded, urging him to move atop her. "Now!"

Landon positioned himself between her legs and entered Raquelle. She gasped as he drove deeply inside her, readjusting to the hardness of him. Reaching for his mouth, they kissed heartily while making love as if the gap for this had never existed.

Raquelle cried out as she had a second orgasm, this one more powerful than the first, while Landon ran his fingers through her hair. Moments later, he inhaled, and his body shook wildly as his own needs came to fruition.

They both rode the wave of sheer carnal delights together, holding each other for dear life till the sensations had waned and they could catch their breaths in the aftermath.

"You were nothing short of amazing," Landon spoke softly as they lay next to each other.

Raquelle flushed. "So were you."

He laughed. "Guess some things in life never change."

"Maybe you're right." *But other things do change*, she thought realistically. Such as the fact that they were no longer married. Or unsure of what this meant for the future between them. If anything at all. "I should probably go," she said, not wanting this to seem awkward as far as sleeping arrangements now that the passion from their intimacy was over.

"Do you have to?" Landon shifted her way. "Stay the night."

"Are you sure?" She met his eyes searchingly. Neither had made any commitments, so there was no more obligation on his part to treat what just happened as a signal than hers.

"I'm very sure," he maintained and kissed her as a stamp of his desire to keep her close at hand till morning.

LANDON WAS UP early the next day after getting little sleep, between a second round of lovemaking to Raquelle—in what turned out to be all-consuming, red-hot sex with his ex-wife—and wondering where they went from here. As far as he was concerned, he would like nothing more than to start dating his ex-wife again, as though for the very first time. Even if they would still need to work through some things that derailed their marriage before, they were given an opportunity to correct the mistakes. Lessons learned, right?

But did Raquelle feel the same way, if not expressing this in so many words?

Then there was the Eddie element that Landon feared could stand in the way of any successful future he and Raquelle might have. Should there be a bad outcome for her brother when the curtain came down, would that shadow hang over them like a sinister presence? Was that something that she could live with and still want to be in a stable relationship with him?

Guess I'll just have to wait it out and not overthink things, Landon told himself as he made breakfast, happy to allow Raquelle to catch up on some sleep before beginning her day.

He had just put some blueberry pancakes on the griddle, recalling that this was something she enjoyed with maple syrup—to go with bacon and coffee—when Raquelle came into the kitchen.

"Hey." Landon grinned when he saw her barefoot and in one of his shirts.

"Hey." She slid a hand through her disheveled long hair. "Hope you don't mind my wearing this. I just grabbed the first piece of clothing I found to see what you were up to."

"I don't mind at all," he assured her. "If the truth be told, the shirt looks much better on you than me."

She blushed. "If you say so."

"I made breakfast—your favorite." Landon grinned as Raquelle eyed the pancakes.

"I can see that." She smiled at him. "Actually, I'm starved. How thoughtful."

"That's just me," he downplayed it. "Have a seat."

Raquelle sat in the kitchen booth and grabbed a piece of bacon off the plate, taking a bite. "I think I could get used to this," she teased him. "Or would that be putting the cart ahead of the horse, considering the fact that we're no longer together?"

Landon put the plate of pancakes before her and said, having pondered this irony himself, "It's not putting the cart before the horse at all. Perhaps it's the other way around and we just needed some time to figure things out."

She looked at him. "And have you—figured things out?"

He kept a straight face when responding levelly, "At least enough to know that what we had has never gone away—whatever that means going forward."

"Hmm." Raquelle was thoughtful as she sliced her knife into the pancakes. "Okay."

Landon sat down and ate with her. He was more than content to leave it at that for now, not wanting to rock the boat by delving too deeply into how their night of mind-blowing intimacy might move the needle in their evolving and rekindling relationship.

Chapter Twelve

The federal raid was about to go down at a warehouse owned by Ivan Pimentel, located on Baldwin Road in downtown Columbia. A tip led Landon to believe that the facility contained stolen and forged art and artifacts in further building the case against the suspected art dealer. It was also suspected that if Eddie were being held captive in relation to the investigation, he could be at that location.

To Landon, it was time to turn up the heat on Pimentel and his crime syndicate. The detailed warrant issued gave them wide-ranging authority in what they could search for and where within the premises. If Eddie could be rescued in the process, all the better. But even without the presence of his CHS, Landon was committed to disrupting the activities of the organization and arresting those perpetrating criminal activity.

The Art Crime Team, armed with Springfield Armory 1911 TRP AOS handguns, were supported by agents with the FBI Special Weapons and Tactics Team, the Bureau's Critical Incident Response Group, and a South Carolina Law Enforcement Division Regional Investigative Unit.

"Let's see what Pimentel has stored inside," Landon said, then gave the order to go in.

After entering the site, prepared for any resistance they

might encounter, they found it was empty, save for a few empty boxes and some trash.

"What the hell...?" Zach uttered.

"Where is everything?" Katie said, furrowing her brow.

"Gone." Landon's voice echoed with disappointment in the warehouse. Including neither sight nor sound of Eddie. "Obviously, Pimentel was given a heads-up and cleared it out—probably with little time to spare—but successfully, nevertheless."

Zach speculated, "Pimentel must be running scared as we close in on his criminal enterprise."

"Either that or he's trying to stay one step ahead of the game," Katie offered.

"I think it's probably a combination of the two," Landon surmised. "Pimentel definitely wants to cover his tracks. But he also knows that the jig is up insofar as his culpability of dealing in stolen and forged art, money laundering and related offenses. He may have pulled one over on us with this obviously staged so-called tip, but his day of reckoning is fast approaching."

They left the warehouse with no more than when they'd entered. Yet Landon was even more determined than ever to see this through to the end, having achieved the desired results. Especially when Raquelle's brother was still missing—but presumed to be alive—and hope remained that he could be reunited with her.

RAQUELLE WAS SEATED in the front row of the auditorium, looking on with approval as the student production was in full swing. She was definitely pulling for the undergraduates someday being able to apply this training to successful careers in theater, films, or television.

Her mind slipped to spending the night at Landon's condo. She blushed at the thought of their hot sex, both giving as much as they took—and more. It truly was as if they had traveled back in time, picking up right where they had left off. Or maybe it was more that the sexual chemistry had simply never wavered, even if they'd been apart for years.

The truth was that sex had never been a problem for them. It was the other things that made a marriage work that failed to measure up to either of their standards. Was it possible that it could be different were they to start seeing each other again in a serious way?

Or was last night—and the mutual satisfaction achieved—merely setting them up for a fall again once the afterglow subsided?

She refocused on the performance. When it was over, she congratulated the students and encouraged them to continue to reach for the stars in their individual goals.

After conferring with Vera on her next class, Raquelle left the auditorium. She was planning to walk over to the nearby Union Building for coffee when someone came up from behind her quickly, grabbing her arm in a rough manner.

"Where is he?" the deep voice asked sharply.

She turned to look at the man. He was staring back at her with solid blue eyes on a square face with a high forehead. Tall and somewhat slender, she guessed that he was in his mid-thirties. While his head was mostly covered with a hood from the blue hooded sweatshirt he wore with jeans and sneakers, she could see that he had thick black hair tucked beneath it.

Raquelle furrowed her brow. "Excuse me?"

"Let's not play games," he hissed. "You're Professor Raquelle Jernigan, aren't you?"

She saw no reason to deny what he obviously knew to be true. "Yes."

"Where's your brother, Eddie?"

He's the man I saw leaving the marina, Raquelle thought as it kicked in like a bad memory. *The one who had to have planted and detonated the bomb.*

"I've been asking myself the same question," she answered, trying to keep her cool as she glanced about in hoping someone would come along to help her get out of this situation. "My brother disappeared—right after someone blew up his pontoon." She peered at the man daringly. "You wouldn't happen to know anything about that, would you?"

He wrinkled his crooked nose thoughtfully and replied ambiguously, "Maybe I would and maybe I wouldn't. What I do know is that Eddie Jernigan is a marked man. He can't escape his fate—if he's not already a dead man—no matter what rock he tries to hide under. So, I ask you again—tell me where I can find him, dead or alive."

Raquelle remained defiant in the face of danger. "Again, I have no idea. But, just for the record, even if I did know something, I'm not about to tell you his location—only so you can kill Eddie."

Still holding her arm painfully, he snorted, "Not the right answer, Professor. I could easily kill you here and now—and would, if there was a price on your head. But here's a warning—unless I can verify very soon that your brother is no longer living, he's not the only one whose lifespan could be cut short in a heartbeat. You pass that along to him. And even the FBI agent he's been giving information to that you were once married to. I'll do whatever I need to in order to satisfy my employer. Think about that!"

Before she could take him up on his threat to her life—not to mention the clear and present danger he was to Eddie…and maybe even Landon—Raquelle found herself being shoved hard enough that she fell to the ground.

By the time she recovered from the shock and got to her feet, the assailant had run off and was darting between buildings on campus to escape.

While shaking like a leaf, Raquelle got out her cell phone from the pocket of her pleated trousers and called Landon.

When he picked up, she said disconcertingly, "I was just attacked by the man who admitted, more or less, to being hired to kill Eddie."

FBI AGENTS AND officers from the Joyllis Hills Police Department joined Braedon College campus police personnel in search of the suspect as Landon and Katie went to Raquelle's office, where she waited for them after her harrowing ordeal.

"Are you all right?" Landon asked first. Never mind that Raquelle had indicated to him over the phone that other than the shock of being pushed to the ground, where she braced herself for the fall—along with the disturbing encounter in and of itself—the attacker had not hurt her.

Raquelle nodded. "I'm fine," she reiterated, standing

by her desk. "At least as much as can be expected after being attacked and threatened by someone."

She regarded Katie, standing beside him, prompting Landon to introduce them. "This is Special Agent Katie Kitagawa," he said. "Katie, my ex-wife, Professor Raquelle Jernigan." He wished she had kept his surname but couldn't hold it against her that she wanted a clean break from him at the time their divorce was settled.

"Nice to finally meet you," Katie spoke in an affable tone while also hinting that Landon had spoken to her about his ex in affectionate terms. "I just wish it had been under better circumstances."

"Me too." Raquelle gazed at Landon with a wry smile.

He kept a straight face when saying, "Why don't we sit down and you can tell us everything you can remember about your encounter?"

"All right." Raquelle sat at her desk, and they sat on accent chairs across from it. She sucked in a deep breath. "He approached me from behind and demanded I tell him where to find Eddie…though seemingly not even sure Eddie was still alive." She paused. "I'm certain—based on appearance and his intimidating words—that he was the same man I saw leaving the marina the day Eddie's boat exploded. When I couldn't, and wouldn't, give him what he wanted, he threatened my life—and even yours, Landon, since Eddie was your CI."

Landon exchanged glances with Katie, then asked his ex-wife, "Did the unsub say who he was working for?" *I'm pretty sure it's Ivan Pimentel*, he told himself but wanted to hear the unsub confirm this in the investigation into Pimentel.

Raquelle shook her head. "Not in so many words. He just described the person as his employer."

Katie leaned forward. "Did the unsub say anything else about Eddie...and his possible fate...?"

"Only that he was determined to find my brother—dead or alive, as he put it—while seemingly implying that time was running out to prove that Eddie was dead."

"In his world as a hired killer, time is always of the essence," Landon suggested. "Meaning that unless the unsub delivers on the contract, his own life may be expendable."

"Or, in other words," Katie threw out, "if Eddie has dropped out of sight, the unsub may well pull out all the stops in trying to locate him...or else—"

Raquelle frowned. "Which still isn't good news for Eddie," she surmised.

Unless he's already dead, Landon thought, well aware that wishing for a favorable outcome alone wasn't always enough to make it come true. "Right now, though, I'm more concerned about your safety. If the unsub was desperate enough to accost you in broad daylight on a public campus, there's a good chance he probably also knows where you live."

"That thought did cross my mind," Raquelle admitted.

Landon told her with assurance, "Until your attacker is taken into custody, I can arrange protection for you." The last thing he wanted was for her to be a sitting duck for a suspected killer—whether on campus or at home. Landon knew she had a top-of-the-line security system in place, but he feared it could still be breached by a determined foe. He stopped short of saying he would be happy to move back in with her temporarily—not wanting it to seem like he was exploiting a vulnerability for something she wasn't comfortable with at the moment.

"Okay," she said simply. "I just hope you can get him—before he finds Eddie."

Katie looked at her. "If the unsub did manage to get off campus, between surveillance video and, if necessary, pairing you with a sketch artist, we should be able to track him down sooner than later…"

Landon was of the same mind. But seeing was believing. Until such time, he didn't want anything to happen to Raquelle. Not when they were just starting to reconnect. They needed time to see if this relationship was real or only a product of weakness that Eddie had inadvertently made possible. It could all still crumble like a castle made of sand, once the case had run its course. With Eddie a casualty for his trouble when the dust settled.

At Helene's Italian House, a restaurant on Gervais Street in the Congaree Vista section of Columbia, Ivan Pimentel sat across the table from his wife, Ava. At forty-seven, she was still as beautiful, slender and loving as the day they met. Married for twenty-five years and counting, they had three children, now all adults and doing their best to make smart choices.

Ivan tried hard not to micromanage their lives, but it wasn't easy. Especially if he felt they were going astray. Fortunately, Ava seemed perfectly capable of using her influence to keep them from falling off the cliff, as it were.

Beyond that, Ivan had more pressing concerns. His hired killer, through Yusef Abercrombie, had failed to deliver on his mission to take out Eddie Jernigan. Or at least that appeared to be the case. But there was still no sign of

Eddie, as though he *had* been eliminated. Or was that a false read that would ultimately come back to haunt him?

Ivan feared that the art dealer stoolie was simply lying low and staying out of sight—perhaps still working with the FBI to bring down his operation. Fortunately, he had tried to stay one step ahead of them. That included clearing out the warehouse of stolen and forged works of art before it was raided by the feds. This gave them less to work with in trying to tie him to federal crimes committed in the art world and beyond.

Still, he needed Eddie Jernigan out of the picture, one way or the other.

If the man who was supposed to make this happen wasn't up to the job, then someone else would be.

"You're not eating," Ava said, breaking into his thoughts as she stopped moving a fork on her plate of chicken fettuccini Alfredo.

Ivan gazed at her face bordered by crimson hair in an angled bob and then at his half-finished veal piccata. He forced himself to slice his knife into a piece and respond tonelessly, "Got distracted. Have things on my mind."

Her eyes widened curiously. "What things?" she demanded.

"Nothing you need to be concerned with," he said, knowing full well that keeping her out of the loop on his illicit activities limited his wife's exposure, should everything ever come crashing down like a rocket out of control.

"I'm always concerned about anything that affects you or our children," Ava told him flatly.

He softened his position, offering her a grin as he said

sweetly, "I know that, and I love you for it. This is just business. Everything will be fine. I promise."

"Okay," she relented and returned to eating.

So did he, washing it down with a sip of red wine.

But just as Ivan was happy to have circumvented the delicate balance between his home and business lives, his cell phone rang. He removed it from the inside pocket of his pinstripe suit coat and saw that the caller was Yusef.

Though he hated to take the call, giving Ava another reason to be annoyed, Ivan knew he had no choice considering the stakes for him at the moment. "I need to get this," he told her and stood, not waiting for a response.

After stepping a few feet from the table, Ivan answered the phone and said irritably, "Yeah?"

Yusef responded bluntly, "We've got a problem."

"What is it?" he demanded, then listened as his assistant gave him some unsettling news pertaining to Eddie and the man who was supposed to eliminate him.

Chapter Thirteen

On Wednesday morning, Landon was pouring himself a cup of coffee in the break room at the field office. Katie had just made herself a cup of green tea, and both of them sat on black stack chairs at a round teak table.

The unsub who went after Raquelle was still on the loose, and Eddie had yet to surface, dead or not.

To say that both situations were stressing Landon out would be an understatement. Compounding this was the fact that the investigation at the center of it all had yet to be completed—leaving the Art Crime Team still on the hook for solving it.

"Your ex is gorgeous," Katie remarked over her disposable paper cup.

Landon grinned. "Tell me something I don't know."

She smiled thoughtfully. "I'm glad her attacker—and alleged bomber of Eddie's boat—didn't hurt Raquelle seriously."

"So am I," he said. "But the fact that he could have—and remains a threat till we find him—still concerns me."

"As it should." Katie tasted the tea. "We'll protect her as long as the unsub remains at large. And beyond, if deemed necessary."

"I know." Landon was comforted by the words, realizing that the Bureau had his back in not wanting a suspected killer putting the family members—or even ex-wives—at undue risk while an investigation was ongoing. "We just need to find the perp. And tie him more definitively to Ivan Pimentel and his crime syndicate."

Katie met his eyes and said confidently, "We will." She drank more tea and waited a beat. "So, is there a real chance you and Raquelle could get back together?"

He stared at the question, giving it all the seriousness it deserved before responding hopefully, "I'd like to think so."

"Good," she said, finishing her tea. "You deserve a second shot at happiness."

"Thanks." Landon couldn't agree more with her assessment. Still, he lowered his own expectations as a defense mechanism toward an alternate result. What he wanted and how Raquelle saw things wasn't necessarily symmetrical. Even if he believed they both wanted to get past his current case and the Eddie factor to see where things stood between them. And beyond that.

IN THE CONFERENCE ROOM, the Art Crime Team assembled with a major development in the case.

Appearing on the large monitor from the FBI Laboratory's Terrorist Explosive Device Analytical Center was bomb expert Joelle Freitas. Thirtysomething, slender, and green-eyed with brunette hair in a ballerina bun, she said measuredly, "Having examined the fragments of the IED that was planted on Eddie Jernigan's Crest Savannah 250 SLSC pontoon, we've learned that the perp constructed a fairly large pipe bomb that was detonated by remote control. We uncovered bomb-making chemicals and components from the boat's remnants, including hexamethylene triperoxide diamine, or HMTD—a highly explosive organic compound—and ammonium nitrate. The bomber clearly meant to destroy the pontoon—and kill anyone on board…"

Landon took note of this and asked, while standing by the screen, "What about DNA? Were you able to collect any from the bomb materials?"

Joelle nodded, pushing up her square eyeglasses. "Yes, DNA, in low levels, was recovered and analyzed," she told him matter-of-factly. "We submitted it to CODIS… and got a hit."

Landon glanced at Zach and Katie. All were eager to hear more with respect to this apparent breakthrough in using the FBI's Combined DNA Index System of criminal justice DNA databases around the country to match an unknown forensic profile from a crime scene to the DNA profile of an arrestee or convicted offender.

Turning back to the criminological scientist, Landon asked anxiously, "So, who are we talking about?"

"His name is Fred Davenport," she replied succinctly. "He's thirty-five and has spent time behind bars for making a school bomb threat and for weapons-related charges."

"Fred Davenport…" Landon muttered to himself. "He's obviously upped his game in going beyond threats to making an actual bomb that he detonated in an attempt to commit murder." *And very likely was also responsible for shooting to death a drifter*, he thought. Along with assaulting and threatening Raquelle.

"Looks that way," Joelle said.

"We'll take it from here," Landon told her then thanked

her for the TEDAC's work in giving them something that represented a turning point in the investigation.

After the video chat ended, Zach, who had a laptop in front of him at the table, said, "I've pulled up Davenport's rap sheet and mug shot."

Katie, seated next to him with her own laptop, stated, "Here's a surveillance camera still photograph of the unsub who accosted Raquelle—and the digital sketch of the suspect that she gave us."

Standing over them, Landon studied the mug shot in comparison with the still pic and sketch. "I'd say they are one and the same," he deduced.

Zach concurred. "Yeah, Fred Davenport seems to be the bomber."

"And obviously still a danger to Raquelle—and likely Eddie as well," Katie said.

"I couldn't agree more," Landon told them, not wanting to give the suspect another opportunity to come after Raquelle, even with an armed marshal staying close to her. "Let's find out where Davenport is living, what he's driving, and anything else pertinent to bringing him in."

RAQUELLE GAZED AT the mug shot of Fred Davenport, the man Landon believed had accosted her. Even in seeing him minus the hood—with dark wavy hair—it was clear to her that this was indeed the person who tried to extract information from her on campus about Eddie. And made threats against her life.

When she texted Landon back, confirming this, he sent her another text stating that Davenport's DNA had been discovered from the bomb materials that crime scene technicians had retrieved from Eddie's pontoon. An arrest of the suspect was said to be imminent.

Thank goodness for that, Raquelle told herself as she sat at the piano. She'd been made to practically feel like a prisoner in her own home, comfortable as it was. Now that appeared to be short-lived. Unless, of course, Fred Davenport somehow managed to circumvent being taken into custody and remained at large.

Then there was still the question of Eddie's whereabouts. Raquelle pushed back the thought that her brother could already be dead—rotting away in a shallow or deep grave somewhere. In the spirit of the Catawbas who had come before her, she had to trust in him that he had found a way to dodge death and would resurface sooner or later.

Until such time, she needed to allow things to play out. Including Landon's art-crimes investigation.

And whatever happened now that their relationship had started to heat up again.

She began to play the piano and glanced at the slender US marshal assigned to her, Julia Ellicott. Pretty and in her late thirties, with blond hair in a short ponytail and blue eyes, she was in uniform and had a weapon in her holster while standing in the great room by the window.

Julia smiled at her and said, "You play beautifully."

"Thank you." Raquelle grinned. "Do you play an instrument?"

"I played the violin in high school—but have been out of practice since then. Maybe I'll take it up again sometime."

"You should," Raquelle encouraged her, believing that everyone should make use of their talents. As opposed to losing them altogether. She thought about Landon's guitar playing and pictured them jamming together—before her thoughts returned to his pursuit of the man who attempted to take her brother's life away at the behest of others.

A WARRANT WAS issued for the arrest of bombing suspect, Fred Davenport, who was considered armed and dangerous—and a BOLO alert for the brown Toyota Tundra pickup truck registered in his name.

While wearing bulletproof vests, Landon and the other armed special agents on the Art Crime Team, along with a SWAT unit, ATF-trained Explosives Detection Canines, and officers from the Columbia Police Department's Fugitive Team, converged on the Sparrow Apartments complex on Platt Springs Road in West Columbia.

After spotting the suspect's truck in the parking lot, they wasted little time before Landon directed them to move in on Davenport's second-story unit. A battering ram was used to enter the two-bedroom apartment. It was sparsely furnished with evidence of weapons, drugs and drug paraphernalia, bomb-making materials—with the K-9s reacting accordingly—on full display.

Once deemed safe enough to move about, they fanned out in search of the suspect. Landon bypassed the primary bedroom when his periphery spotted something in a bathroom. With his gun drawn, he entered and spotted a fully clothed man lying on the floor in his own blood. A bullet wound in his temple oozed more blood.

Landon recognized him as Fred Davenport, while taking note of the firearm that was lying on the tile floor beside the bathtub. He recognized it as a Korth 2.75-inch Carry Special .357 Magnum handgun—the type of weapon used to shoot to death drifter Lim Ramírez.

When Katie and Zach stepped inside the bathroom, Landon had already determined that the suspect was dead and told them at first glance, "Looks as though Davenport, sensing the walls were closing in on him, decided to take his own life—"

"Too bad," Katie said, frowning. "Would have loved to get him in an interrogation room to hear what he had to say about Ivan Pimentel."

"Unfortunately, dead men can't talk," Zach remarked suspiciously. "A bit too convenient, don't you think?"

"It does raise more questions than answers," Landon conceded. Not the least of which was whether or not looks could be deceiving in the fatal scenario before them. And what Davenport's death said or didn't say about Eddie's status. Or being able to effectively connect the dots between Davenport and Pimentel and his criminal organization under investigation for art theft and forgery.

UPON SECURING A search warrant, after the body was removed by the Lexington County Coroner's Office, evidence of criminality was seized from Fred Davenport's apartment. This included a cache of firearms and ammunition, two jars of HMTD, pipes used to make bombs, and illegal narcotics.

As far as Landon was concerned, Davenport had clearly equipped himself with the means to carry out future small- and large-scale bombings in addition to the use of handguns to complete assignments as a hired gun. But his murderous ways had taken a big hit with Davenport's own life ending mysteriously.

Had he truly chosen to check out before they could arrest and interrogate him? Or had the bomb-and-murder suspect—and Raquelle's attacker—been silenced in the same way that Eddie might or might not have been?

Landon wrestled with these questions in his office as a video chat request came on his laptop. He saw that the caller was Nancy Kincaid, a physical scientist from the FBI Laboratory. She had been sent the handgun Davenport allegedly killed himself with and ammo from it to compare with the weapon and bullets used to kill Lim Ramírez.

He accepted it and said, "Hey."

Nancy, who was in her forties and had short brunette ombré hair, gazed back at him with aquamarine eyes and responded, "Hey. Got something for you…" She took a breath. "The Korth 2.75-inch Carry Special .357 Magnum handgun, ammo, and spent shell casing that you sent to the lab were tested. They matched perfectly with the three bullets and shell casings fired from the gun barrel—with five lands and grooves and a right-hand twist—of the weapon that killed Lim Ramírez. It was the same revolver," she emphasized.

"Figured as much," Landon said, sitting back. It lent credence to Davenport using the same gun he murdered Ramírez with to shoot himself. Or was it only made to look this way by someone hoping to tie up loose ends? One in particular. "Did you submit the firearm ballistic evidence into the NIBIN database?" he asked, using the acronym for the ATF's National Integrated Ballistic Information Network that contained digital ballistic imaging info on gun-related crimes for cross-referencing across the country.

"Yeah, we did." Nancy smiled. "The gun was traced and originally purchased legally in Huntington, West Virginia, three years ago. It was reported stolen the following year and used eight months ago in a drive-by shooting in Greensboro, North Carolina, which left a teenaged victim in critical condition—but he survived."

"Okay." Landon didn't necessarily believe that Davenport was the culprit or gun thief, suspecting that he had purchased the gun on the black market without asking questions that would never be answered truthfully—and added it to the firearms collection he had amassed as a gun for hire. Along with being an improvised bomb maker and user.

The important thing was that it linked the Korth 2.75-inch Carry Special .357 Magnum revolver to two deaths—both related to Eddie Jernigan's disappearance—and ostensibly the art-crimes case against Ivan Pimentel.

RAQUELLE WAS RELIEVED with the news that the man suspected of bombing Eddie's pontoon and accosting her, Fred Davenport, was now dead—an apparent suicide victim. She was admittedly surprised that he would rather die than be held accountable for what he had tried to do to her brother. Somehow in her brief interaction with him, Davenport had struck her as a man full of himself and not one to make it easy for the authorities by taking himself out of the equation.

But then again, what did she know?

"Hope we never have to see each other again," Julia Ellicott told her lightheartedly when the U.S. marshal had been cleared to end the bodyguard assignment.

Raquelle chuckled. "Me too."

"You have a nice day." Julia smiled at her. "And keep playing the piano."

"I will," she promised and saw the marshal out.

After changing into exercise attire and tying her hair up, Raquelle went out for a run. The freedom of being in the woods and in touch with nature was something she never wanted to take for granted. Any more than the sanctity of life. Or how it felt to be loved when she and Landon were married. Could they get back there again?

When she got back to the house, Raquelle phoned Landon for a video chat. Her face brightened when she saw his handsome features appear on the small screen. "I was wondering if you'd like to come for dinner this evening," she asked him without prelude.

His eyes lit up. "Of course I would."

"Great." She grinned thoughtfully. "See you at seven thirty."

"Count on it," he told her, and they left it at that.

Raquelle grabbed her handbag and popped over to the store to pick up a few items. Afterward, she took a shower, put on a fresh set of clothes, and went to the kitchen to prepare a traditional Native American meal. It included roasted duck, wild rice with berries, vegetable soup, cornbread, and Indian pudding. She would serve sweet wine to wash it all down.

When Landon arrived, looking dashing in his clothes, she greeted him warmly. "Glad you could make it."

"Wouldn't want to be anywhere else," he insisted, sporting a wide grin.

And I wouldn't want you to be anywhere else, Raquelle admitted to herself. "Dinner's ready."

Landon sniffed in the scent of food and declared, "Smells tantalizing. Can't wait to eat."

She smiled. "It won't be long. Make yourself at home."

In her mind, Raquelle didn't imagine that would be too difficult, as this place would always belong to both of them. At least in spirit.

Soon, they were seated on upholstered tufted chairs at an acacia-wood rectangular table in the dining room.

"How do you like it?" Raquelle asked hesitantly, knowing just how long it had been since she cooked him a meal.

Landon regarded her while eating and waited to clear his throat before responding, "This is incredible. I love your cooking—always have." He broke off a piece of cornbread. "Trust me when I say you haven't lost a step in the kitchen."

She had to laugh. "You think?"

"Yeah, I do," he reiterated, putting the cornbread inside his mouth. "Guess I just needed to be invited to remind me of what I've been missing."

Raquelle blushed. "I think that goes both ways," she confessed, using a spoon to scoop up soup. "We gave up a lot—without fully realizing it—till it was too late…"

Landon met her eyes. "I did realize it," he told her in earnest. "Just wasn't sure how to get it back—or if we ever could."

"Hmm…we'll see about that." She wasn't sure where to go from there. But was more than open to seeing if they could learn from their mistakes and make up for them.

"Good." He sliced a knife into the roasted duck and switched subjects. "We've been able to tie the revolver that killed Fred Davenport to the gun used to kill Lim Ramírez in the woods near Eddie's apartment. It's a good bet that Davenport targeted the drifter, believing him to be Eddie."

Raquelle cocked a brow. "After he failed to blow up Eddie with his boat?"

"Yes, looks that way."

"And all to keep Eddie from spilling the beans about wheeling and dealing in stolen and forged Native American art?" she asked in disbelief, rolling her eyes.

"That appears to be the size of it," Landon said firmly, then sipped his wine. "Ivan Pimentel has blood on his hands, in more ways than one. We're very close to making him pay for this, along with his cohorts."

"That's good to know." Raquelle tasted her own wine musingly. "And what about Eddie? Will we ever know what happened to him? Or hear from him?" The thought of being left hanging for the rest of her life was unsettling to say the least.

"Yes, to both." Landon lifted a forkful of wild rice with berries. "I'll make it my business to get to the bottom of his whereabouts—and help you to deal with it one way or the other."

"Thank you." It was the most she could expect from him, knowing full well that he was as frustrated as her. And as determined to know the truth about her brother.

After having Indian pudding with another glass of wine, Landon got up abruptly for a trip to his personal vehicle. He returned with a guitar case and said, "I thought if you were up for it, we could play the guitar and piano together like we used to."

Raquelle beamed. "Sounds great to me." She was delighted to see if they were as in sync today as when married. Something told her that would be no more of a problem than in bed, where they picked up so easily from where they left off.

When the music ended satisfactorily, Raquelle invited Landon to her primary suite. She watched as he assessed the large room with its rustic decor and furnishings as though for the first time.

He turned to her and said, "It's nice—but you were always the main attraction for me in this room."

"Ohh..." She colored, feeling flattered. "Let's see just how long it takes for that sentiment to come back to you," she dared him as the desire to be intimate again had her totally at his beck and call.

He kissed her deeply and said with desire, "I promise, not long at all."

Landon didn't disappoint as they made love and went the extra mile in pleasing one another, as if to put an exclamation mark on their heated chemistry and making up for lost time.

For her part, Raquelle knew that she was falling in love again with her ex-husband. Assuming she had ever truly fallen out of love with him. The only question was whether that was enough to leave everything on the table in wearing her heart on her sleeve while letting bygones be bygones.

She fell asleep on that note, safely tucked in Landon's arms.

Chapter Fourteen

"Happy birthday!" Landon voiced to his mother on a cell-phone video chat as he stood inside his condo. He'd left Raquelle's place an hour ago, after having breakfast together like old times, to get ready for work.

Zelda Pritchard had turned sixty but could easily have passed for a woman ten years younger. Thin, she had chestnut hair in a layered, short cut and the same gray eyes that had been passed down to Landon.

Her face brightened as she said, "Thank you, Landon." She became thoughtful. "I'm so glad to have reached this point in my life."

He took that in multiple ways. One was reaching sixty while finding later success as a real estate agent. Another was knowing that his father, William Briscoe, had not even reached age forty before disaster struck. Finally, the fact that she was happy to celebrate her birthday with a new husband—Chuck, a retired neurologist—to share her life with as they settled into a place in the Blue Ridge Mountains of Tennessee.

I can't take any of that away from her, Landon thought, knowing she deserved every bit of happiness that he wanted for himself. "So am I," he told her, grinning. "How's Chuck?"

"He's doing well," she said.

"Great." Landon waited a beat to then say what was likely to come as a shock to her, "I've started seeing Raquelle again."

Zelda lifted a brow. "Really?"

"Yeah." His voice was mellow. "It's true."

"And how did this come about?" she asked curiously.

"It's a long story," he answered, meditative. "No time to go into details just yet. Suffice it to say, though, I can only hope the story has a happy ending."

"So do I." Zelda flashed her teeth with encouragement. "You two made a great couple. No reason that you can't again."

Landon grinned. "I couldn't agree more."

He almost hated to cut the conversation short but knew that if things went his way there would be plenty of time to discuss his revived relationship with Raquelle. Which would open the door to reestablishing their own connection and even his getting to know Chuck better.

Landon headed out to the field office, expecting the autopsy report to come in at any time now on the circumstances surrounding the death of Fred Davenport.

KATIE RODE WITH Zach as they drove into Saluda Shoals Park in Columbia, having taken the west entrance on Bush River Road. They had been surveilling, while keeping their distance, a black BMW X5 M SUV with Ivan Pimentel and Yusef Abercrombie inside.

After the BMW parked, Pimentel and Abercrombie got out and headed into the riverfront park. Katie and Zach left his vehicle and trailed them.

"Something tells me they're not out for a leisurely stroll

in the park," Katie said humorlessly, carrying a powerful zoom digital camera for official work.

"No, not likely." Zach grinned. "Let's find out what they're up to."

"All right." She hoped the art-crime suspects might give them even more to work with in solidifying a case that was unshakable.

They watched as Pimentel and Abercrombie made their way to the river observation deck, where they were joined by another man.

Zach asked intently, "Who's that?"

"I'll get a closer look," Katie told him. They were on the opposite side of the river, while hidden from view, amid southern sugar maple trees and red buckeye flowering plants. Using the zoom lens, she homed in on the trio. And then, more specifically, the unknown male. He was white, in his mid-forties, tall and of medium build, and had brown hair in a bun. She recognized him as wanted international art smuggler Hans Duey, who had also been on their radar and specialized in Native American stolen art and artifacts—selling them to the highest bidder. Duey had been fingered by Eddie Jernigan as part of the Art Crime Team's transnational investigation.

"That's Hans Duey, who Pimentel and Abercrombie went out of their way to meet with," she said matter-of-factly.

"Not too surprising," Zach said knowingly. "The trio are likely trying to get their stories straight while hoping to stay one step ahead of the law."

"Good luck with that," she said sardonically while snapping pictures and recording video of the three men conversing. "Aside from adding more fuel to the fire for our case, our partners at Homeland Security Cultural Property, Art, and Antiquities Investigations will love this—as part of their overall goal to dismantle global crime syndicates and their trafficking of cultural property for money laundering and funding of their various criminal activities."

Zach paced and responded conclusively, "You're right—we're on the verge of holding Pimentel and his associates accountable for their transgressions. Whether or not that includes the death of Eddie Jernigan is still up in the air."

Katie was of the same mind. She continued to hold out hope that Eddie was somehow able to sidestep the worst outcome for his disappearance. If only for Landon—and his resumption of romance with Raquelle.

LANDON WAS AT his desk as Lexington County Coroner's Office Deputy Coroner Jeannie Estrada appeared on the screen of his laptop. Fortysomething, she was on the slender side and had short, straight brown hair with blond highlights and brown eyes.

She smiled. "Afternoon, Agent Briscoe."

"Afternoon," Landon said anxiously. "What did you come up on with on the death of Fred Davenport?"

Jeannie went right into business mode as she responded in a measured tone of voice. "We've completed the autopsy on Mr. Davenport. Though the preliminary exam suggested that his death may have been a suicide, we now believe the decedent's death was a homicide…"

"Is that so?" Landon cocked one brow. "Why the change of heart?"

"The initial observation was never meant to be the official cause of death," she defended the coroner's office. "It was only after conducting a complete autopsy that we were able to ascertain that, in fact, the decedent was shot at close range by another person—and it was made to look like a suicide."

"Hmm…" Landon gazed at her with interest, knowing that this played into his own strong suspicions that Davenport was taken out to silence him. Much like they had tried to do with Eddie—and might have succeeded as well. "Go on," he nudged her.

Jeannie nodded and said, "There was some deep bruising on the shoulders of the decedent to suggest that he was being held down by someone—or possibly more than one person. The blood patterns on his arms indicated that they were raised in an upward position after death. Pretty hard to pull off for a dead man acting alone," she uttered wryly. "Finally, the placement of the gun on the bathroom floor indicated that Davenport would've used his right hand to shoot himself in the temple. Problem is there were no lacerations or abrasions on the decedent's index finger that normally would be present when one fired a weapon. Hence the final conclusion is that the manner of death was murder by a single shot to the head, causing significant damage that proved to be fatal."

"Not surprising that we're talking about a homicide here," Landon had to say. "Makes sense when coupled with some other factors in our investigation. What's the estimated time of death?" he asked for context in gathering evidence on the crime and those involved.

She gave a two-hour window but cautioned him, "It could have come a little earlier or later."

Close enough to work with, Landon told himself. Then he said to her routinely, "I understand."

After ending the video chat, he went to brief the special agent in charge, finding her in the field office's gym.

Shannon, keen on fitness, was moving briskly on a treadmill when Landon walked up to her. "What do you have for me?" she asked assumingly.

"Just got the autopsy report on Fred Davenport."

"And...?"

"Turns out, he was murdered—not a suicide." Landon watched her reaction. "The Korth 2.75-inch Carry Special .357 Magnum revolver that killed Davenport was the same handgun used to shoot Lim Ramírez."

Shannon's eyes widened. "You think someone else killed Ramírez?"

"I think Davenport was hired by Ivan Pimentel—or more likely, his right hand, Yusef Abercrombie—to blow up my CI's boat," Landon told her, laying out the facts again as he saw them. "Bomb-making materials discovered in Davenport's apartment corresponded with those used to construct the IED placed on the Crest Savannah 250 SLSC vessel. When Eddie managed to escape the explosion, by all accounts, I believe that Davenport—needing to complete his assignment—shot to death Ramírez, mistaking him for Eddie. But then Davenport himself became a loose end that needed to be taken out of the equation."

"Hence using his own weapon to make it appear that he shot himself—allowing Pimentel and company to wash their hands of a hit gone wrong," Shannon ascertained, using a towel to wipe perspiration from her face.

"That's how I see it," he said in agreement. "But it backfired, as we now know that Davenport was murdered with a firearm—from his own stockpile of weapons—and Eddie may well still be a thorn in Pimentel's side."

"So, what's the next move in piecing this together?" she asked impatiently.

"We try to find surveillance videos or cell phone information that can place one of the suspects at or near Davenport's apartment around the time of death—to go with any forensic evidence we can gather." Landon jutted his chin. "While also moving progressively on the case we've built against Pimentel's crime organization on stolen and forged Native American artwork." *And hope Eddie is still able to provide us with more intel on the criminality*, Landon told himself.

"Good." She drew a breath. "By the way, in case you hadn't heard, HSI CPAA investigators picked up fugitive art smuggler, Hans Duey—after Zach and Katie made him while Duey rendezvoused with Pimentel and Abercrombie at Saluda Shoals Park."

"I knew about the meeting," Landon said, having been brought up to speed by Katie. "I'm glad to hear that Duey's been arrested. Homeland Security can keep him on ice while we make the case in tying our investigations into cultural property thefts and trafficking together."

"Exactly." Shannon offered him a smile, then resumed her workout. "Keep me posted."

"Always." Landon grinned. He walked away, thinking, *We'll get this done and arrest the culprits and make it stick*. Even while the current state of affairs for Eddie remained a conundrum.

RAQUELLE WALKED INTO Deirdre's Coffee Bar on Knotter Marina Drive. She had been invited there by Eddie's former girlfriend, Penelope.

It occurred to Raquelle that maybe her brother had reached out to Penelope, who would then convey a message to her. At least to say that he was safe. Perhaps far away from the coffee bar on beautiful Lake Owenne, where she was now standing.

Or was she getting carried away by expectations that might fall flat?

"Hey," Penelope greeted her warmly.

Raquelle smiled. "Hi."

"Thanks for coming."

"Not a problem," Raquelle assured her. "I was done teaching classes today."

"All right."

They headed for the food service and then beverage station. Raquelle went with fresh coffee and a brownie while Penelope got a matcha and a vegan scone.

"There's a table by the window," she said and ushered Raquelle in that direction.

They sat with a nice view of the lake. The boats dotting it asymmetrically beneath sunshine reminded Raquelle of when she would go out with Eddie on his pontoon. She would give anything to do so again. Perhaps with Landon—and maybe even Penelope, if she were so inclined.

"So, have you heard from Eddie—or anything more about his disappearance?" Penelope asked casually after nibbling on her scone.

Raquelle met her eyes, hiding disappointment, as she responded truthfully, "I was about to ask you the same thing." She paused, tasting the coffee. "Sorry. I know that you and Eddie are no longer together—so thinking he might have contacted you again…"

Penelope made a face. "About that. There was something weird—or maybe not really—that happened a couple of days ago…" She sipped her green tea. "I got a call from someone with no caller ID. I could hear breathing, but the person never said a word—before the call disconnected… Strange, huh?"

Raquelle's jaw dropped as she asked what they were both apparently contemplating, "And you think it might have been Eddie calling you…?"

"Truthfully, the thought did cross my mind." Penelope sighed. "But if it was him, why didn't he just say so?"

Good question, Raquelle thought, breaking off a piece of her brownie. She could only hope that the caller was Eddie, which would mean that he was still alive. And not buried somewhere that they would never find him. She gazed at Penelope and responded musingly, "Maybe Eddie had second thoughts about materializing…or coming clean about where he's been hiding or his current whereabouts." Raquelle paused. "Could be that he simply wanted to protect you from being targeted by those who are targeting him—"

Penelope peered at her. "What did he do so wrong that someone would want him dead?"

"I've asked myself the same thing," she confessed, even when she knew that her brother had apparently stepped over the line in supplying Landon with intel that was damaging enough to want both payback and the crime syndicate's attempts to protect their interests by taking Eddie out of the picture. But since the case was still under investigation and a sensitive subject matter, she couldn't be specific. "All I can say is that Eddie stepped on the toes of some very bad actors, metaphorically speaking, by doing his part to stop Native American artwork from being stolen or forged. Now he's paying the price."

"I hate that." Penelope ran a hand through her hair.

Raquelle twisted her lips. "Me too."

"So, I take it you haven't heard from him either?" she asked. "At least so you were able to have a conversation?"

"I wish." Raquelle sighed and lifted the coffee mug. "There's been no contact since Eddie left me a voicemail the day his boat was blown up. I'm trying not to read too much into that—such as his being unable to communicate because he's dead—but I do wonder what's going on. And if there can still be daylight at the end of the tunnel for my brother."

Penelope leaned forward and said ponderingly, "Maybe Eddie is trying to protect you too by being deliberately uncommunicative and staying out of sight."

"I've considered that," Raquelle said, sipping the coffee. If so, why keep Landon at arm's length and unable to provide assistance? "But it still doesn't make the not knowing any easier to stomach."

"I get that." Penelope put a hand on hers. "I'm sure your ex-husband and the entire FBI are doing what they can to find Eddie and get some resolution to this."

"They are." Raquelle smiled tenderly, fully aware that Landon was as committed as her to solving Eddie's disappearance. As well as holding those responsible for this and the pontoon explosion totally accountable. "So, where did things go wrong between you and Eddie?" she asked curiously.

Penelope bit into the scone, while staring at the question posed. After a moment or two, she answered evenly, "Like other couples, I suppose we pushed each other away for reasons that were probably not worth fighting over, much less breaking up." She took a breath. "If he gets through this, maybe we can talk about getting back together."

"That would be wonderful." Raquelle couldn't help but smile at the prospect. Having experienced firsthand how two people could find their way back to one another again, she had hope for Eddie and Penelope. But first her brother needed to be all right. And if WITSEC were to be a factor, maybe the two of them could start over together. Or was it feasible that an archaeologist and art dealer of different tribes could put everything behind them for all the right reasons?

Raquelle drank more coffee and pondered this…as well as her own future possibilities with Landon.

While wearing a cap and dark sunglasses, Eddie watched inconspicuously as Raquelle and Penelope left the coffee bar and walked along the dock. They exchanged a few more words and embraced like lifelong friends before going their separate ways.

He tried to decide which one he should follow. His exgirlfriend? He still longed for a second chance with and had wanted to communicate this to—then thought better of it for her own sake.

Or his beloved sister? Choosing to keep her in the dark was one of the hardest things he'd ever done. But knowing full well the lengths his pursuers would go to in order to silence him forever was more than enough to want to keep his distance from Raquelle. That included by phone or computer—both of which could be intercepted by those who were capable of that sort of thing.

The last thing he wanted was for Raquelle to become a target too. She had a good life, and he didn't want to mess with that. Besides, he knew that Landon would have her back, no matter where things went from here for all three of them.

Eddie watched again from his position on the dock as both Raquelle and Penelope headed for their vehicles. He wisely chose to leave both of them alone. Should he survive this crisis borne of his own making, there would be time to try and fix everything he had broken.

He walked away, making himself scarce again with the constant threat of death and disaster following him around like the Grim Reaper.

Chapter Fifteen

Landon played the guitar for Raquelle that evening. He was at her place, feeling very much like he belonged there once again. But never taking it for granted that this was where he was meant to be. He wanted Raquelle—and more than just to share the same bed with. They had come to terms with their past mistakes and were seemingly ready to explore a new beginning, where new memories could be created.

I won't try to get it all back at once, no matter how comfortable things seem between us, Landon told himself. He was standing in the great room, as was Raquelle, while strumming the guitar, which she seemed riveted by. *I can play all night if it makes her happy*, he thought as a grin spread across his lips.

Each holding glasses of wine, they settled onto a modular sectional sofa that had an Indigenous custom-made slipcover on it. Landon thought it was a good time—or bad, depending on how you looked at it—to tell her about the most recent developments in the case. Whether he liked it or not, Raquelle had skin in the game, thanks to Eddie's involvement.

"So, as it turned out, Fred Davenport didn't take his own life," Landon said with a catch to his voice. "He was shot to death in a deliberately staged suicide, according to the coroner's office, following the autopsy on Davenport."

Raquelle cocked a brow. "For what purpose—to make it seem like he acted alone in blowing up Eddie's boat?"

"I'd say it was more a half-hearted attempt to throw off the art-crimes investigation and take the onus off the main players in the game," Landon told her matter-of-factly. He tasted the wine. "Instead, it shows the desperation and the lengths they are willing to go to in order to conceal their criminal behavior. Quite the contrary, as another homicide has been added to the investigation." In so saying, Landon realized that it brought them back to Eddie and his invisibility. He truly regretted recruiting Raquelle's brother as his CI—though it made sense at the time, for him and Eddie. But now, with his former brother-in-law still unaccounted for, he was an elephant in the room that figured to remain part of the picture so long as Eddie's situation remained unresolved.

Raquelle sipped her wine, thoughtful. "I think Eddie is still alive—and may have contacted Penelope…"

"Really?" Landon was anxious to hear more. "Explain."

Raquelle sighed and said, "Two days ago, someone with no caller ID phoned Penelope. Though she could hear breathing on the line, the caller never spoke before ending the call. She thought it might have been Eddie reaching out—but backpedaled instead."

"Interesting…" Landon drank more wine as he assessed this. It would obviously mean that Eddie was alive and able to communicate from a position of safety. "What do you think?"

Raquelle met his gaze and answered pointblank, "My

gut tells me it was Eddie on the phone. He's out there—somewhere—and trying to find his way back. But may not be sure how."

"You could be right." Landon sat back. "If it was Eddie, he has my number—and yours. We have to believe that he's smart enough to push past any uncertainties and reach out to those in the best position to help him extricate himself out of this mess—before it's too late..."

She nodded and tasted her wine. "I do believe that. Eddie has to know we're on his side. When ready, he'll make the call and do what he needs to do to reclaim his life."

"Okay." Landon put his arm across her shoulders, pulling them close together, while hoping her faith in Eddie would be justified. The harsh reality was that Ivan Pimentel still viewed Eddie as a major obstacle to his criminal enterprise and wanted him dead—even if Fred Davenport was no longer around to get the job done.

ON FRIDAY MORNING, Landon got a call from Detective Spencer Davidson.

"Hey," he said curiously. "What's up?"

"Just wanted to get back with you on the drifter, Lim Ramírez, shot to death in the woods..." Spencer drew a breath into the phone. "As the current theory is that it was a targeted hit—though apparently the wrong target—we came across some surveillance video a few blocks away from the crime scene that should interest you..."

Landon asked, definitely piqued, "What's on it?"

"The footage clearly shows Ramírez being stalked by another man," Spencer replied. "For how long, who knows? But this proves, if nothing else, that it wasn't a random murder. Ramírez was followed to the woods with the intent on assassinating him—believing him to be your CI, Eddie Jernigan, if what your investigation has put together is on the money."

"It is," Landon assured him. "All the pieces fit—including the resemblance between Eddie and Ramírez as well as the proximity to Eddie's residence. And the fact that the murder occurred shortly after an IED was detonated on Eddie's pontoon. Ramírez was simply in the wrong place at a convenient time for the killer. I believe the video will confirm that to be Fred Davenport, who was himself gunned down—"

"What's that they say about you reap what you sow?" Spencer's voice lowered an octave. "Must have been karma or something."

"Yeah, perhaps." Landon didn't necessarily buy into that line of thought, but Davenport might well have signed his own death warrant by, it seemed, failing to put Eddie out to pasture. "Send the video."

"On its way," the detective said.

When he opened it on his cell phone, Landon could see Ramírez wandering aimlessly. He was followed by a man wearing a hoodie, with the hood over his head. After freezing the frame and zooming in on the stalker, Landon believed it was the same person who had attacked Raquelle.

Fred Davenport.

To Landon, it was yet one more piece of the puzzle that wound its way right back to Ivan Pimentel and his desire to stop Eddie from providing any further intel into Pimentel's criminal activities.

At 11:00 A.M., Yusef Abercrombie was brought in for questioning as a person of interest in the investigation of Fred Davenport's murder.

In a windowless interrogation room, Landon sat on a metal chair at a wooden table, across from the seated suspect. He wasted no time going after him, placing a photograph before Abercrombie of a deceased Davenport.

"Do you recognize him?" Landon asked with an edge to his voice.

Abercrombie glanced at the picture and replied smugly, "Should I?"

"Yeah—his name is Fred Davenport." Landon jutted his chin. "Two nights ago, he was shot to death in a bathroom at his apartment in West Columbia—but it was made to look like a suicide."

"And this has to do with me, how?" The suspect appeared unflappable as he sat back in his chair.

"Since you asked," Landon said sarcastically, "he's the guy who was hired to blow up a boat at Knotter Marina that was supposed to have art dealer Eddie Jernigan on it when the explosion occurred. But he wasn't, fortunately. Still, Jernigan is now missing. In the meantime, Davenport has kicked the bucket himself. I don't suppose you know anything about either of these things…?"

Abercrombie frowned and said sneeringly, "You're right, I don't. Eddie Jernigan is someone my employer, Ivan Pimentel, has done business with. Other than that, I know nothing about his boat. Or what might have happened to him." Abercrombie sighed. "As for this Fred Davenport, the name doesn't ring a bell—"

"Well, maybe I can help it to ring inside your head," Landon told him. "A surveillance camera was able to place a BMW X5 M SUV registered in your name to within two blocks of Davenport's apartment—where he was shot—around the time of his death. Can you explain this?"

The revelation seemed to catch Abercrombie off guard. He took a long moment before answering. "Though it technically belongs to me, the BMW you refer to is actually a car that is routinely driven by different people who work for Mr. Pimentel, in conducting business involving his art galleries and related interests. So, I'm sure you will find that the BMW was driven by one of these employees during the time that you say it was in the area you speak of."

"We'll see about that," Landon tossed out, doubting his story. "But was someone else also using a cell phone in your name, which pinged near the apartment complex where Davenport lived at around the time of his death?"

Landon strongly suspected that Abercrombie, on Pimentel's orders, had been dispatched to take out Davenport—while making it appear to be a suicide. Moreover, it seemed that as Pimentel's wingman, Abercrombie had likely been the one to hire Davenport as a hit man. Cell phone records would probably show communication between the two men—before Davenport became expendable after botching the job, as now appeared to be the case.

Abercrombie looked to be stumped trying to weave his way out of this one. His brows knitted thoughtfully before he responded. "I'm the only one who uses my cell phone. When you say, 'near the apartment complex,' I don't know what that means. I spend a lot of time in and around West Columbia—for both business and pleasure.

If my cell phone pinged in the vicinity around that time, it was purely coincidental, nothing more." He kept a straight face. "Sorry to disappoint you, Agent Briscoe. If you expected a confession, I'm afraid it's not happening."

Actually, I wasn't expecting an admission of guilt, Landon told himself. That would be way too easy. No, if they were going to hang one or more murders on Pimentel and Abercrombie—to say nothing of the myriad art-related crimes they were believed to have perpetrated, along with accomplices—it would need to be proven in a court of law. With solid evidence to back it up.

Gazing across the table, Landon said coolly, "I'll need a list of any other employees of Ivan Pimentel who may have been driving the BMW during the time in question—"

"I can do that," Abercrombie said, looking pleased with himself. "No problem."

"Okay." Landon glanced at the video camera that was showing the interview to Katie and Zach in another room. "You're free to go."

"Thanks."

Before Abercrombie could get up, Landon said to him for a reaction, "By the way, you and Pimentel were spotted by FBI agents at Saluda Shoals Park—meeting with known art smuggler Hans Duey. He was taken into custody on international charges. Do you have anything to say about that?"

The man scratched his chin ponderingly. "Only that we met with Hans as someone we believed to be a legitimate art dealer," he argued. "If he did anything illegal, I can assure you that Mr. Pimentel played no part in it. Neither did I."

Yeah, right, Landon thought, finding the notion laughable at best. And appalling at worst, considering the transnational crimes they were believed to have committed. Not the least of which was murder. And there was still Eddie's status to be determined categorically.

"Thanks for your time," Landon said, then saw Abercrombie out the door.

The suspect turned to Landon and stated, looking him in the eye, "As I'm sure you realize, Agent Briscoe, being under investigation is not the same thing as being guilty of any alleged crimes…"

I'm pretty sure the two go hand in hand in this case, Landon told himself but responded intently, "You're right about that. But just so you know, a criminal investigation may also prove the guilt is real—when the verdict comes in…"

Abercrombie bristled at the thought and walked away.

When Katie and Zach came out of a viewing room, Katie said, her brow creased, "Can you believe him? Abercrombie must think we're totally stupid. The man's lying through his teeth—about pretty much everything."

Zach concurred. "We should've just arrested him on the spot—with Pimentel following in his footsteps on solid RICO charges, at the very least."

"I agree," Landon told them. "But it made more sense to let him sweat it out a little longer. Pimentel too, while giving them more rope to hang themselves. Meanwhile, let's keep an eye on Abercrombie. Something tells me that beneath the cool-as-a-cucumber facade, he's a rather loose cannon that Pimentel isn't afraid to utilize in whatever way he sees fit."

RAQUELLE SAT IN the auditorium, offering a few comments and words of encouragement as her student actors performed on stage. Each clearly took their roles seriously, wanting to both please her and use the opportunity as a stepping stone for their future aspirations in the entertainment industry or otherwise.

I only wish I had been as gung-ho in what I wanted to do with my life when I was in college, Raquelle thought enviously as she sat next to the Department of Theatre Chairperson Yves Deutschman. She glanced at him. In his sixties, he was rail-thin and had silver hair in a short fringe style and a Balbo beard. His gray-blue eyes were focused on the performers.

Raquelle turned back to the stage. Though she had generally been career-oriented through the years, having a family was every bit as important. She understood that now and hoped it might actually become a reality, seeing that her one true love, Landon, was back in her life. And he seemed to want the same thing as a future parent who could introduce his progeny to his own mother and stepfather.

That family also extended to her brother, Eddie, who was out there somewhere, being chased by bad guys. He would have to stop running at some point and let them in.

At least Raquelle wanted to believe this. Her biggest fear was that he would run out of time and those out to get him would be successful, thwarting Landon's efforts to hold them accountable for any art crimes they committed.

Raquelle pushed that thought aside and applauded when the performance was over. As the students high-fived each other, knowing that they had aced it, possibly surpassing even their own expectations, Yves bellowed excitedly, "Bravo, bravo!"

Raquelle laughed. Naturally, she had to follow suit—keenly aware that it would reflect well on her—by mimicking him, "Bravo!"

At that moment, her cell phone buzzed. Raquelle removed it from the pocket of her bouclé jacket. She saw that the caller was Jay Locklear, Eddie's friend from the reservation.

Getting up from her seat, Raquelle walked down the aisle, away from the stage, and answered the call. "Hey, Jay," she said attentively.

"Eddie was here," Jay spoke tonelessly.

"Really?" She composed herself. "When?"

"Since shortly after his boat exploded," he responded matter-of-factly.

She lifted a brow. "But you claimed Eddie wasn't there when Landon and I came to the Catawba lands…?"

"I know." Jay took a breath. "Eddie asked me not to say anything if anyone—including you—came looking for him. Since it wasn't my secret to tell, I respected his wishes."

Though Raquelle understood his loyalty to her brother—and breathed a sigh of relief in knowing that Eddie was indeed alive—she had to ask, ill at ease, "So, why are you telling me this now?"

"Because Eddie's left the reservation," Jay replied. "He didn't tell me where he was going—though I gave him some money to work with—and I didn't ask. But I thought you deserved to know at least that much."

"Thank you, Jay," Raquelle expressed sincerely.

"Hope Eddie gets everything straightened out," he stated.

"We both do," she told him.

Raquelle added Landon to that list as well. Knowing that removing himself from the sanctuary of the reservation meant that Eddie had once again placed himself in danger. Assuming he had chosen to return to Falona County and the line of fire, bombings, and gunshots aimed squarely at him.

Chapter Sixteen

On Saturday morning, the FBI Art Crime Team's dedicated special agents were on the verge of raiding a storage facility rented by Ivan Pimentel on Atlas Road in Columbia while executing a search warrant for stolen and counterfeit Native American art. They were backed by detectives from the Columbia Police Department's Investigations Division.

Landon suspected that Pimentel had emptied out his warehouse downtown on Baldwin Road and hidden whatever he could that was illegal in the storage unit—while waiting for the heat to die down.

Dream on, Landon thought with sarcasm, knowing that the heat was about to get much hotter for the crooked art dealer as the investigation moved toward its conclusion.

He recalled the day before when Raquelle shared the news that Eddie had been holed up at the Catawba Nation reservation. Eddie had apparently been spooked enough after his pontoon was blown up to feel that his safest bet was to duck out of sight somewhere Ivan Pimentel and associates would be least likely to be welcomed in trying to locate him.

While Landon was certainly glad to know that Eddie had survived more than one attempt on his life and was apparently still standing, he wasn't as thrilled at the notion that Raquelle's brother had vacated the shelter of the tribal lands for places unknown.

Had he thrown caution to the wind and returned to Falona County?

Would Pimentel get word that Eddie was still alive—assuming it had ever been believed to be otherwise when no proof of death was presented by Pimentel's hired bomber—and seek to finish the job with a new assassin?

Where are you, Eddie? Landon asked himself. Would his CI reach out to him for help before the clock stopped ticking?

Raquelle was asking herself the same question. While Landon had deployed all available resources to try and locate Eddie, his former brother-in-law had proven to be quite adept at doing a disappearing act. But how much longer could his luck hold out—when someone with financial muscle and self-interests wanted him dead?

Landon gave the go-ahead to break the lock on the storage unit door.

They went inside and, as expected, saw that the large space was filled with artwork and artifacts.

Wearing nitrile gloves, Landon began to sift through the items. He asked, "See anything that catches your eye as recognizable or suspicious?"

Katie responded, "Yeah, here's something—"

With her own gloved hands, she held up a Native American work of art that Landon recognized from the National Stolen Art File as having been swiped from an art museum in Kentucky. "Looks like the real deal," he remarked.

"If not, it's a great counterfeit painting," she said. "Either way, it will still work against Pimentel."

"I agree," Landon said.

Zach told them, "We've got more art theft to work with…"

They looked as, wearing gloves, he lifted up two more paintings that were on their radar from intel provided by Eddie.

Landon flashed a half grin with approval as he discovered another hidden gem that fell within their purview and said, "Looks like we've hit the proverbial jackpot here—adding to the strong evidence we already have—in our bid to outmaneuver Pimentel and put his racket out of commission for good."

LATE THAT AFTERNOON, Raquelle went for a run on the trail through her property. She felt a mixture of emotions. There was the fact that Eddie was still breathing, answering one prayer. But keeping him alive would likely take more than prayers alone. Landon and his Art Crime Team would need to find and protect her brother—something that had already proven to be easier said than done.

I have to believe that having survived this long, Eddie can come out of his ordeal stronger than ever, Raquelle told herself, feeling the tension in her quads and calves as she pushed herself.

Then there was the situation with Landon. Apart from the totally in sync lovemaking that left her continually wanting more, Raquelle knew she loved him. And sensed that he loved her again. But he hadn't expressed as much. And neither had she. Was that some sort of omen that it

might not be in the cards after all for them to give it another try?

*Or am I totally misreading the signs that should be
telling me we really are onto something in this resur-
rection of our romance*, she mused as she headed back
to the house.

After getting a bottle of water from the fridge and
downing one-third of it, Raquelle was ready to hop into
the shower when her cell phone rang. She removed it from
the pocket of her shorts and saw that the call was coming
from someone with no caller ID.

Instinctively, as she remembered Penelope receiving
such a call with no response, Raquelle answered it and
asked guardedly, "Eddie...?"

It took a moment or two before the caller responded,
"Yeah, it's me."

"Where are you?" she asked, heart pounding.

"Meet me on the pier at the Knotter Marina," Eddie
said tersely. "Come alone..."

"Okay," she replied without hesitation.

Before Raquelle could pepper him with more questions and get some needed answers, the phone went dead.

A WARRANT FOR Ivan Pimentel's arrest was issued—along
with his crony, Yusef Abercrombie. Both were facing a
slew of art-crime-related charges, supported by the evidence. That included a direct link to Fred Davenport
and the bombing of Eddie's Crest Savannah 250 SLSC
vessel after intel obtained from Davenport's laptop indicated that he was indeed working on behalf of Pimentel—
having been hired by Abercrombie—to blow up the pontoon with Eddie aboard.

Landon was also prepared to charge both men under federal law with murder and conspiracy to commit murder in the deaths of Lim Ramírez and Fred Davenport. Abercrombie's alibi and attempt to throw others under the bus fell flat once DNA evidence proved that he had been inside Davenport's apartment—the bathroom where his body was found, in particular—while doing Pimentel's bidding to eliminate a person who could tie them to the two attempts on the life of Landon's CI.

A BOLO alert was sent out for the crooked art dealer's white Mercedes-Benz GLE 350 4MATIC SUV. Simultaneously, FBI agents were raiding Pimentel's local art galleries and his gated luxury estate on Cedarwood Lane in Columbia.

As Landon drove down the street in his Chevy Tahoe, he thought about Raquelle and wanting to put it all out there about how much he still loved her and wanted them to make this work—the second time around. Did she feel the same way? Would she be just as committed to meeting him midway, while doing whatever they needed to mitigate—if not get past altogether—the issues that worked against them previously?

I'll just have to go for it, Landon told himself, feeling reasonably confident that they were meant to be. Even if Eddie's circumstances continued to be in flux, Landon believed that he and Raquelle were on solid enough ground to be able to withstand anything that might present itself as they navigated the road ahead.

When a call came in from Katie, Landon put his cell phone on speaker and set it in the dashboard phone holder. "Yeah," he said.

"Abercrombie was somehow able to give the agent tailing him the slip," Katie said sorrowfully, "before he could be taken into custody. We put out a BOLO alert for his BMW X5 M SUV that appeared, at last sighting, to be headed toward Knotter Marina Drive."

Landon sighed, wishing he'd gone with the strong circumstantial evidence they had to keep Abercrombie off the streets as a serious person of interest. "I'm not far from there," he told her. "We'll get him—and Pimentel—before they can do more damage."

"We'd better," she cautioned. "As if there's any other choice…"

"There are no other choices," he concurred, eager to see this investigation come to a head one way or the other.

After Landon disconnected, he opened the voicemail Raquelle had left him while he was talking to Katie. He listened with interest as Raquelle spoke tensely:

"Landon, I got a call from Eddie. He wants to meet me at Knotter Marina and asked me to come alone. I agreed out of fear that he might bolt again if he saw you—other FBI agents or law enforcement… I'm on my way there right now. I'll do my best to keep him there—till you arrive…to help Eddie and hopefully he'll be able to help you in return—to make all this worthwhile for both of you—"

Landon muttered under his breath, rattled by this turn of events. He would have preferred that Raquelle had given him a heads-up before she went to meet her brother rather than on her way. But knowing how much Eddie's predicament and absence had unnerved her, could he really blame Raquelle for jumping at the opportunity to do what she felt was right in helping her brother?

At least she let me know what's happening, Landon

told himself, *and is counting on me getting there to save the day for her and Eddie.*

Problem was Raquelle might have placed Eddie—and herself—in more danger.

Landon considered that Yusef Abercrombie also seemed to be headed on a beeline toward the marina. Had he been following Raquelle? Or perhaps put a GPS tracker on her car in hopes of being led right to Eddie— so he could finish him off once and for all?

Landon called Raquelle to warn her about the impending threat posed by Abercrombie, but it went straight to voicemail, where he left a message. This did little to ease his own discomfort that she was about to be put in harm's way. The thought that he might never get the chance to convey his true feelings about her and them shook Landon to the core.

He passed the information to Katie and Zach, directing them to get a SWAT team and other law enforcement to the marina ASAP.

In the meantime, Landon pressed down on the accelerator as he sped toward Knotter Marina, knowing full well that every second counted with two lives very much hanging in the balance.

EDDIE STOOD ON the dock walkway, tilting his cap lower to cover his face more, while wondering if Raquelle would show up. Admittedly, he had a lot of explaining to do and probably not much time to do so. But what could he say, really? And how? That he'd gotten in over his head in selling counterfeit art to make ends meet? Or had tried to turn the page by being Landon's CI?

Everything he had tried had ended in disaster. Or close

to it. Including being targeted by the crooked art dealer and galleries owner Ivan Pimentel as a snitch, in paying a ruthless hit man to blow up him and his boat.

This brush with death freaked Eddie out like no one would believe. Seeing his life flash before him as though it were someone else's had forced him to go into hiding, knowing his future was very much in jeopardy—were it up to Pimentel and his lap dog, Yusef Abercrombie, to decide whether or not he lived or died.

If given another opportunity, Eddie hoped he could somehow make amends for his missteps. Pay his debt to society without spending time behind bars. Or was it too late for that, now that he had violated the conditions Landon had set in being his confidential human source?

Eddie fidgeted as he waited for Raquelle, his gaze through sunglasses searching the area for any sign of her. He hoped she did as he asked and came alone. Now was not the time to have to deal with Landon, whom Eddie was certain had reentered his sister's life during his disappearance. This was probably a good thing. Raquelle hadn't really been herself since their divorce. If his ex-brother-in-law could make her happy, then so be it.

At the moment, though, Eddie had more pressing concerns and was growing increasingly uneasy about coming out of hiding and exposing himself to further danger.

Chapter Seventeen

Raquelle was a bundle of nerves as she reached Knotter Marina and found a place to park. She wondered if Eddie had stayed put or if he'd been scared off by real or imagined threats and bolted away, leaving her in the lurch.

I can't miss out on the chance to communicate with Eddie and convince him to work with the FBI again for his own protection, Raquelle told herself. She left the car and headed for the pier. *He has to be here*, she thought, moving briskly down the dock walkway and scanning past the boats lining it, while noting that another boat was now in place where Eddie's Crest Savannah 250 SLSC pontoon had been. The image of it bursting into flames before her very eyes flashed in Raquelle's head like a bad dream. As horrible as it was, the fact that Eddie had escaped made it somehow bearable. Except that she sensed he still had an X on his back and, as such, was not out of the woods yet.

She took out her cell phone and saw the voicemail from Landon, who undoubtedly would not have approved of her going solo to meet her brother. Maybe it wasn't the smartest thing to do, with Eddie wanted by both the FBI (as a CHS vulnerable to the whims of some bad actors) and those wanting to silence him for good.

But I had to go with my gut instincts on this one,

Raquelle mused, sure Landon would understand and respect that. She listened to the voicemail:

*"Raquelle, thanks for letting me know that Eddie's
alive and well—and wants to meet you at the marina.
I'd strongly advise that you wait till I get there. I think
someone may have put a GPS tracker on your car, hoping to be led to your brother. If so, it could place you both
in danger. Call me when you get this message. I'm on my
way there. Please, be careful..."*

Raquelle considered whether or not Fred Davenport
might have placed a GPS tracker on her Infiniti when he
was lurking around the vehicle on campus—with those
responsible for Davenport's death now being able to track
her whereabouts in search of Eddie.

Should I go look for it on my car? she asked herself,
sighing.

While grappling with that and about to call Landon
for further clarification, Raquelle heard a familiar voice
say in an uneven tone, "You came..."

She turned to see Eddie standing there. He was wearing a blue cap and dark shades along with a brown cor-
duroy shacket over a white crewneck T-shirt, jeans, and
black hiking shoes. He was sporting a five o'clock shadow
beard on his face.

"Of course I did," she told him levelly, as though he
had given her a choice.

"Thanks." His eyes darted in both directions ner-
vously. "Let's walk...away from everyone...and then
we can talk."

"Okay." Raquelle walked beside him toward the end of
the pier that extended out onto the lake on both sides. It allowed them a bird's-eye view of others coming and going.

For now—not wanting Eddie to freak out if she called Landon to tell him where they were—Raquelle put her cell phone back inside the pocket of her slim jeans. They were worn with an almond-colored chenille sweater and comfort shoes. She had her hair in a low ponytail.

Removing his sunglasses, Eddie regarded her and asked casually, as if a routine conversation starter, "So, how have you been?"

"Worried to death about you," Raquelle said, meeting his brown eyes squarely. "More than once—with zero communication between us after the boat explosion—I feared you were dead."

"I get that," he muttered. "My bad. I'm sorry I put you through everything that I did."

"I'm just glad you're all right." She decided with a once-over that he didn't appear to be the worse for wear in spite of living life on the run. "Why did you drop out of sight instead of contacting me or Landon for help...?"

Eddie's shoulders slumped. "I really screwed up," he offered contritely. "Made some bad choices that I wished I could take back. That includes selling some Native American art that I knew wasn't legit—but I needed the money. When Landon offered me a way out by becoming his CI and being let off the hook—I took it." He sucked in a breath. "But after the people I was working with discovered I was feeding Landon information, they came after me. When I was nearly blown up with my pontoon, I panicked—not sure if there was a mole within the FBI or who I could trust... I didn't want to get you involved and become a target too, so I fled—"

"To the rez," Raquelle finished his story. "Jay called me." When she saw Eddie furrow his brow, as if this was an act of betrayal, she told her brother, "He was worried about you—and felt I had a right to know, after visiting the reservation in search of you."

"I know," he spoke equably. "I saw you there, with Landon—but I just wasn't ready to see either of you at that time."

She gazed at him, questioning. "And you are now...?"

"Yeah. I was tiring of having to continuously look over my shoulder." Eddie's chin jutted. "I want my life back and am prepared to tell Landon everything I know and give him what I've gathered to make his case against a dirty art dealer and his associates. But first, I needed to see you to try and explain what happened—if you'd let me..."

"I'm glad you did, Eddie—and thank you for coming back to the surface." Raquelle's eyes welled with tears, and she hugged her brother.

"Love you too, sis," he spoke emotionally, hugging her back.

She looked him in the eye and said straightforwardly, "Now, we need to get you out of here. Landon thinks that a GPS tracker may have been put on my car, meaning I could have been followed here by—"

Eddie said swiftly, "We'll take my car..."

"Okay." Raquelle didn't bother to ask where he got the vehicle, knowing that his Audi Q4 Sportback e-tron had been impounded by the authorities as part of the investigation into his disappearance. Beyond that, she was sure that Landon would soon be at the marina to assist in getting Eddie out of harm's way. But perhaps not soon enough for them to wait it out.

They left the pier and were headed down the dock

walkway when they were suddenly approached by a tall and bearded thirtysomething man who was stocky and had black hair in a hipster fade style and dark eyes. Raquelle noted that he was holding a gun with a silencer—and pointing it at Eddie.

"You're a hard man to track down, Eddie—or should I call you *snitch*?" the man said in a deep and hardened voice.

Raquelle turned to look at her brother, who responded tartly, "Guess you just didn't try hard enough, Yusef."

"You know him?" She eyed Eddie and then the other man.

"Yeah. His name's Yusef Abercrombie," Eddie answered matter-of-factly. "He works for Ivan Pimentel, the dirty art dealer who wants me dead."

Both names rang a bell to Raquelle as she'd heard them mentioned more than once by Landon in regards to Eddie missing in action and the art-crimes investigation. "This can't be happening," she thought out loud.

"I'm afraid it is." Abercrombie peered at her, then turned to Eddie. "Welcome back from the should-be dead," he said sarcastically. "The man I hired to get the job done was an utter failure. My mistake. He's left me to do the dirty work for him—and clean up his mess…"

Eddie sneered. "So, what, you plan to shoot me here at the marina, where any and everyone can see…?"

"If I have to," Abercrombie retorted, then glared at Raquelle. "Your sister will be the first to take a bullet if you fail to cooperate, Eddie. I have no qualms about killing her, trust me."

"Just let her go," Eddie pleaded with him. "It's me that you want—and here I am."

"Yeah, here you are." Abercrombie regarded him with contempt. "Unfortunately, you don't get to call the shots. We're all going to leave the marina together. Once we get where we're going and you give us what we want, only then can your sister—Professor Jernigan—walk away..." He shot her a cold stare. "The choice is yours, Eddie..."

Raquelle was under no illusion that Abercrombie had any intention of letting her—much less, Eddie—come out of this alive to talk about it. As she was now a victim of their abduction and witness to Abercrombie's plans to murder her brother, there was no way Ivan Pimentel's enforcer would ever leave her to implicate them in Eddie's murder.

I have to try and buy some time, Raquelle told herself as she glanced at her brother, who had been put in an almost impossible situation that she was at least partially responsible for.

She fixed Abercrombie's face and asked pointblank, "How did you find us anyway? Was it the GPS tracker that Fred Davenport—your hired assassin—put on my car...?" She watched as Abercrombie reacted with surprise as to her knowledge of this, thanks to Landon.

"You know about that, huh?" Abercrombie made no attempts to deny this. "Since it makes no difference at this stage—yeah, I took ownership of the tracking device in hoping to locate your brother—once Davenport's services were no longer needed."

"So, it was you who killed him with his own gun while trying to make it look like Fred Davenport died from a self-inflicted shot to the head?" Raquelle pressed and thought, *Keep him talking.*

Abercrombie laughed. "Guess the cat's out of the bag

now—thanks to Agent Briscoe and his ties to both of you." He kept the gun aimed at them. "Davenport's repeated failures to do what he was paid to do—starting with taking out a stoolie by blowing up his boat—left me with no choice but to remove Fred from the picture—permanently. Now, enough of this chit-chat. Let's go..."

As they proceeded down the walkway, Eddie was clearly hoping to find a way out of this. He said brusquely to their abductor, "Killing me—us—won't change anything. The deed is already done. The FBI has more than enough to put you, Ivan, and others involved in art theft and forgery away for a long time. You'd be smart to just give yourself up."

"You'd like that, wouldn't you?" Abercrombie chuckled wryly. "Not going to happen. The way I see it—and Ivan feels the same way—without your testimony, the case falls apart and we walk. Not too complicated."

It's complicated enough, given the multiple dead bodies they would leave in their wake, Raquelle thought, herself included among the casualties. She mused about the Witness Security Program possibility that had been mentioned for Eddie as a means to escape being prevented from ever testifying. Of course, it would never come to pass should Abercrombie get his wish to take her brother's life beforehand.

"You'll never get away with this!" Raquelle snorted at the man with the gun, wondering what move she should try to break his concentration should all else fail. She suspected Eddie was contemplating this as well, knowing that once they left the marina there would be no turning back for either of them.

Abercrombie replied confidently, "Watch me!"

She took that for what it was worth and, at the same time, caught some movement around the marina—people swiftly going this way and that—clearly indicating something was up. This clued Raquelle in on the assumption that law enforcement was on the scene—now catching sight of Landon, in particular—and determined to stop Abercrombie from carrying out his murderous plans.

LANDON SPOTTED RAQUELLE and Eddie as they were being led by Yusef Abercrombie at gunpoint across the dock. Obviously operating on behalf of Ivan Pimentel, Abercrombie intended to kill both Eddie—as an FBI CHS with damaging intel on their criminal enterprise—and Raquelle, who could identify Abercrombie.

I'm not going to let that happen, Landon told himself. Raquelle wasn't going to finally be reunited with her brother, only for the two of them to end up murdered.

Not to mention Landon had other plans for his ex-wife that required that they both lead a very long life—with a family thrown into the joyful mix for good measure. No one would take that away from them. Least of all the man who murdered Fred Davenport after the bomber of Eddie's boat was unable to complete the assignment that would have ended Eddie's life.

Landon scanned the marina, where he saw FBI snipers positioned with Rock River Arms LAR-15 assault rifles and ready to take out Abercrombie on orders to do so. Meanwhile, Katie and Zach were in the process of bringing in Pimentel for his various crimes of art theft and forging Native American art as well as orchestrating the plot to murder Eddie—on at least three different occasions—and Raquelle.

Having evacuated the marina or issued shelter-in-place orders for as many as possible under short notice, it was time to move in on Abercrombie. Landon could only hope that this ended without Raquelle or Eddie getting hurt.

With his own weapon drawn, Landon waited as the trio moved down the walkway. He then blurted out, "Yusef Abercrombie, I have a warrant for your arrest. Drop the weapon and put your hands up."

Instead of doing that, Abercrombie suddenly grabbed Raquelle around her neck and put the barrel of his gun up to her temple and said defiantly, "No can do, Agent Briscoe. You and the other agents are going to let the three of us leave here. If anyone tries to stop us, your ex-wife's brains will be splattered onto your CI's face, and that'll be on you—"

Eddie tried to intervene. "Leave her alone, Yusef. I'll take Raquelle's place, and you can do what you and Ivan have been planning to do all along."

Abercrombie kept the gun on Raquelle and said, "Nice try, but something tells me I'm much better off at the moment with her than you—no offense." He glared at Landon. "What's it going to be, Agent Briscoe—deal or no deal…?"

Landon had no intention of risking Raquelle's life by taking one good shot at Abercrombie, no matter if he hit the mark. The downside was far too great. On the other hand, from another vantage point, Matthew Ricci, a forty-five-year-old experienced sharpshooter for the FBI SWAT team was wholly reliable in eliminating the threat, if need be.

Just as Landon was about to give the go-ahead to take out Abercrombie, Eddie suddenly lunged toward him.

This caught Abercrombie off guard, and he pointed the weapon at Eddie. Raquelle got in on the action when she slammed a solid fist in Abercrombie's right eye.

He screamed in agony and while he was trying to decide who to shoot, Ricci beat him to the punch—firing a single shot that was deadly accurate—hitting Abercrombie squarely in the forehead. The suspect went down like a failed rocket after its launch, dead on arrival. The gun separated from Abercrombie's grasp, landing harmlessly next to him.

Only then did Landon rush over to them, putting his own gun back inside the holster. He regarded his CI and said, "Good to see you again, Eddie."

Looking a bit frazzled but clearly counting his blessings, Eddie responded tentatively, "Yeah, you too."

Landon gave him a pat on the back and turned to Raquelle. He hugged her, not wanting to let her go but forcing himself to do so. "I was afraid I might lose you for a moment there."

"So was I," she admitted. "But it didn't happen, thank goodness."

With a slight smile, he asked her, "Where did that punch come from?"

"Somewhere deep inside me, itching to come out at an opportune moment." Raquelle drew a breath, glancing at Abercrombie, who was lying there awkwardly. "He had that coming to him," she declared.

"At the very least," Landon concurred while thinking appropriately, *And then some.* He gazed at Ivan Pimentel's right-hand man and the firearm he fully intended to use to kill Raquelle and Eddie. Landon recognized it as an FNX-45 Tactical semi-automatic pistol, equipped with a suppressor. He wondered if Abercrombie had used the weapon under Pimentel's authority to finish off others in his criminal orbit that broke the rules.

As members of the Bureau's Critical Incident Response Group and South Carolina Law Enforcement Division Regional Investigative Unit took over, Landon told Eddie, "I'll need you to come to the field office to give a statement on what you have for me and have been up to lately—"

Eddie nodded. "I can do that," he said. "I borrowed my friend Rex Shepherd's Mitsubishi Outlander. I'll follow you there."

"Okay." Landon was glad that the bartender had Eddie's back in his time of need. Just as he himself had Raquelle's back every step of the way.

"I'd like to be there with Eddie," she said, eyeing Landon.

Though he fully understood where she was coming from in wanting to support her brother, Landon had to say in response, wanting to keep this as professional as possible, "I think it's best that I speak with him alone."

Raquelle nodded acquiescently. She squeezed her brother's hand. "Everything will be all right."

Eddie met her gaze contemplatively. "Yeah."

Landon felt the same way, more or less, optimistic that they had cleared a major hurdle with Eddie still around to help secure the case against Ivan Pimentel. This notwithstanding, he was well aware that they still had some hoops to go through and potentially treacherous roads ahead.

Chapter Eighteen

"First, I have to say, Eddie, that we're glad to see you sitting across this table," Landon said sincerely while Zach stood in a corner of the interview room and Shannon and Katie watched in the viewing room. He was sure that his CHS was nervous after everything that had gone down. But they needed to know what he knew—and how he'd managed to get out from under a real threat of death that led to three others losing their lives. "So, tell me why you decided to drop out of sight?"

Eddie ran a hand through his hair, which had grown a bit since before the explosion, and responded matter-of-factly, "After someone planted a bomb on my boat and waited to see me die there, I panicked." He sucked in a deep breath. "I wasn't sure who I could trust—so I bolted to give me some time to think."

Landon peered at him and stated unequivocally, "You could trust me. I've always been straight with you." *At least to the extent possible without compromising the investigation*, he told himself.

"I know." Eddie sat back. "It was just hard to deal with having a target on my back."

"I understand." Landon leaned against the table. "So, how did you manage to get off your pontoon before it blew up?" he asked curiously. "Were you tipped off some-how?" Landon couldn't rule out entirely that there could have been a mole within the Bureau—or from an outside source in the criminal sphere with a vested interest in pro-tecting Ivan Pimentel's racket in the art world.

Eddie pinched his nose for a beat and then responded straightforwardly, "I saw a man on the dock who I thought I'd seen before—talking with Ivan and Yusef. Though I tried to duck out of sight, I could swear that he looked right at me. He walked by my boat harmlessly enough, making me have second thoughts that he was out to get me." Eddie sighed. "Still, I had a bad feeling that some-thing was about to go down. I just knew that I needed to get off the boat. You know what happened after that…"

"Yeah." Landon showed him a photograph of Fred Dav-enport, unsure just how much Eddie was privy to while being in seclusion. "Is this the man you saw at the marina?"

Eddie took a hard look at the picture and said suc-cinctly, "That's him."

"Fred Davenport planted the bomb on your boat," Landon said and got a reaction from Eddie. "He was killed by Yusef Abercrombie."

"I heard about that," Eddie said thoughtfully. "Guess he became expendable too."

"True. But not before Davenport shot to death an in-nocent man—mistaking him for you," Landon told him candidly.

Eddie furrowed his brow. "I'm sorry someone else got swept up in all this," he muttered.

"Me too." Landon took a breath. "Unfortunately, it happens. Especially when a hired killer knows no bound-aries."

"So, what now?" Eddie met his gaze. "Am I in trouble for violating our agreement by skipping out on you?"

Normally, Landon might have felt that once a CI had reneged on his or her undercover role, all bets were off regarding any consequences that might be rendered. But in this instance, running for one's life was not a crime, in and of itself. Quite the contrary, anyone might have done the same under similar circumstances, with their back to the wall. But Eddie had returned—and in one piece.

Then there was the fact that as Raquelle's brother, Landon couldn't throw the book at Eddie. Not if he wanted to win her over and chart a course that they could both live with.

"You're not in trouble, Eddie," Landon told him and glanced at the video camera and those watching them. As his own CHS, there was some leeway on how far one could use discretion in the course of an investigation. "The intel you've provided has been, for the most part, useful in the case we've built against Pimentel and his cronies. Now that you've been made, I'm not expecting you to go back in—only to be taken out by someone else—with Abercrombie having failed in this endeavor, along with Davenport."

"About that…" Eddie reached into the pocket of his shacket. He pulled out a flash drive. "While still on the inside, I collected as much additional info as I could on stolen genuine Native American artwork and forgeries that Ivan got his hands on—names, dates, photographs, places, profits, deliveries, and more… I hung on to it as an insurance policy—if my life or Raquelle's was on the line and all else failed…"

Landon was handed the flash drive. Based on what

he'd just heard from Eddie, he suspected that it could well contain enough intel to ensure that in combination with other hard evidence, Pimentel was put away for a very long time. Being able to tie the crooked art dealer directly to Davenport with Eddie's eyewitness account was a further reason for optimism that the case against Pimentel was solid.

Unfortunately, it also meant that this gave Ivan Pimentel more motivation for still wanting Eddie dead.

Landon knew this was another major crisis point that would need to be addressed.

AFTER DISCUSSING THE latest twists in the case with the Art Crime Team and briefing the special agent in charge, Landon headed to Raquelle's house. He was happy that she had her brother back—at least for now—and they themselves could move forward in hopefully setting the stage for a future together.

When pulling up to the property, Landon noted the black Mitsubishi Outlander that belonged to Eddie's bartender friend parked in the driveway. *Looks like Raquelle already has company*, Landon thought, not too surprisingly, circumstances being as they were.

Raquelle opened the front door as he walked up to it and said softly, "Hey."

"Hey." He grinned, happy to see the glow in her beautiful face.

After Landon stepped inside the great room, she told him, "Eddie's taking a shower. I've invited him to stay in one of the guest rooms for now, as his apartment is still in shambles."

"That's a good idea," Landon spoke supportively.

"With a great security system, this is a much better bet for Eddie at the moment." The long term would take more consideration.

"So, how did the interview go?" she asked curiously.

"Good. Eddie laid out the sequence of events that led him to flee and remain at large for as long as he had. All satisfactory, as far as I was concerned."

Raquelle smiled. "I see."

He added, "Eddie also handed over some important intel related to the investigation that he obtained while working as my CI, and had held on to for safekeeping, that had been on his boat just before it exploded."

"Something they were hoping to find when they ransacked his apartment?" she deduced.

"That would be my guess," he concurred, given the high stakes at play for Ivan Pimentel in his efforts to avoid arrest and prosecution.

Raquelle was thoughtful. "Would you like something to drink?"

Tempting as it sounded, he declined. "I have to get back to the investigation," Landon said. "Besides, you need to spend some quality time with your brother." *And vice versa, after what Eddie has been put through*, he thought.

She started to object but seemed to appreciate the gesture. "All right. Thanks."

Landon smiled. "I'll call you."

"Okay."

He was about to leave then abruptly turned to face her, knowing that one thing needed to be said here and now. "I love you."

Raquelle's eyes lit up. "You do?"

"Yeah," Landon had no trouble admitting. "I never

stopped loving you, in spite of everything that went awry between us."

She held his gaze for a moment, before stating, "I love you too, Landon."

He felt a warmth in his heart in that moment that nothing could replace, prompting him to cup Raquelle's cheeks and plant a quick but decisive kiss on her soft lips.

Then he left, already plotting strategy for what came next.

RAQUELLE TOUCHED HER mouth that still tingled from the kiss. She truly did love Landon. Hearing that he felt the same way brought her untold joy and a belief that their relationship had taken a big step in the right direction— wherever they landed.

She was seated at the island on a beige faux-leather bucket stool when Eddie came into the kitchen. He was cleanly shaven and wearing a fresh set of clothes.

Raquelle flashed a smile. "Hey."

"Hey." He sat beside her.

There was a bottle of beer and plate of store-bought oatmeal-raisin cookies on the counter before him.

"I heard the interview with Landon went well," Raquelle said, lifting the mug of coffee she'd made for herself.

"Yeah." Eddie grabbed the beer and drank some. "I'm just glad to finally put everything out on the table and let the chips fall where they may."

"If all goes well, those chips will fall right on top of Ivan Pimentel's head," she stated humorlessly.

Eddie chuckled and lifted a cookie. "Landon seems to believe that."

"He only wants to solve the case—while minimizing collateral damage." *Meaning harm to you*, Raquelle told herself. Beyond what had already occurred.

"I get that." Eddie ate more of the cookie while regarding her. "So, what's happening with you two?" He glanced toward the great room, where Landon's guitar was in its case against the wall. "Looks like Landon's been spending some time here."

Raquelle saw no reason to hold back. "Yes, we've started seeing each other again."

Eddie grinned. "Figured as much." He sipped beer, musing. "Hope it works out this time around."

"Me too." She picked up an oatmeal cookie and nibbled on it.

"You deserve to be happy," he told her. "Both of you."

"So do you, Eddie," Raquelle said thoughtfully. "Penelope has been worried about you. We've been in touch ever since—"

"I know." Eddie tilted his face. "I saw you both at the coffee bar."

She gazed at him. "You were there?"

"Yeah, close enough." He sighed. "Wanted to reach out, but wasn't quite ready to at that time."

"I understand." Raquelle rested her arm on the counter. "You need to let Penelope know you're all right—assuming she hasn't already heard on the news. I wanted to tell her but thought it would be better coming from you directly."

"I'll go see her," he promised.

"Okay." She paused. "I think she still cares about you."

"Seriously?"

"Yes, if I'm reading her correctly. Maybe you two can also make it work the second time around."

"Yeah, maybe." Eddie put the beer bottle to his mouth, pondering.

Weighing on Raquelle's mind was how such a rekindled romance might play out if he was put into WITSEC. Could keeping Eddie alive ruin any chance of him getting back together with Penelope?

ON SUNDAY AFTERNOON, Landon sat beside Katie in an interrogation room. On the opposite side of the table sat Ivan Pimentel and his lawyer, Ashley Vasquez, of Sarchuk, Vasquez, and Norgaard LLC, a top law firm in Columbia. In her early thirties, she was slender and attractive with sable hair in a stylish pixie cut with amber eyes behind heart-shaped glasses.

Wearing an orange jumpsuit, Pimentel had shown little interest in communicating with them without the presence of his attorney, as was his right. But it also showed Landon that the conniving and vindictive art dealer knew that he was in big trouble and was hoping that he could somehow worm his way out of this hole of his own making.

Landon peered at the suspect and stated bluntly, "I'm not going to beat around the bush, Pimentel. We've built a strong case against you for numerous federal offenses—including the buying, selling and trafficking of counterfeit and stolen Native American works of art, wire fraud, and money laundering. As if that's not enough—and it isn't, trust me—there's conspiracy to commit murder, attempted murder, two actual federal murder charges, and various offenses related to the use of an improvised explosive device by someone you hired. In short, you're looking at a very lengthy prison sentence…"

Pimentel shot him a wicked glare before whispering into his attorney's ear. Then he said coldly, "Your so-called strong case is built on a mountain of lies. I'm a successful art dealer who has done absolutely nothing wrong."

Katie pitched in, saying derisively, "You can claim innocence till you're blue in the face, Pimentel, but it won't change the facts any. We're not messing around here— even if you are."

He scowled at her and was about to offer a retort, but Ashley Vasquez checked him and said with a sigh, "This is really getting us nowhere, Special Agents Kitagawa… Briscoe. My client and I maintain that this entire thing is a fishing expedition at best and a case chock full of unproven holes and innuendoes at worst."

Landon eyed the attorney and Pimentel sharply and responded without humor, "Not much for fishing, I'm afraid. But I can assure you that most of the holes in this case have been filled—by your client and his underlings. That includes Yusef Abercrombie—who took a fatal bullet to the head for his boss, Pimentel. But not before Abercrombie confessed to doing his dirty work in hiring Fred Davenport to plant a bomb on a boat belonging to art dealer, Eddie Jernigan—and then shooting Davenport to death for falling short in the attempt at murder—"

Ashley pursed her thin lips and locked eyes with Landon as she retorted, "With all due respect, Agent Briscoe, as both Mr. Abercrombie and Mr. Davenport are no longer here to defend themselves, your accusations can hardly go unchallenged—and we will challenge them, vigorously. What I can say is that anything Abercrombie did outside the law, he did on his own and it had nothing to do with my client or Abercrombie being on his payroll."

"Keep telling yourself that," Katie voiced glibly. "Maybe even you will start to believe it."

Pimentel's brows knitted when he stated with an edge to his tone, "Regarding Eddie Jernigan, whatever he went through, he brought upon himself by being a snitch. Not very smart. Apart from that, anything Jernigan passed along to you was nothing more than misinformation— and even planted fake evidence—all so the FBI can try to make a case with no foundation whatsoever!"

Landon figured Pimentel was trying to push their buttons but was in fact sweating bullets inside as he had to know that this would not go his way at the end of the day. That included Eddie's testimony, intel, and evidence obtained—more than enough to seal the deal. So long as he stayed alive and well till Pimentel's trial.

"Looks like we've reached an impasse," Landon told them. "More or less."

"Appears that way." Ashley grinned triumphantly. "As such, I think we're through here, Special Agents. We'll see you in court."

Landon nodded. "That you will," he promised.

"That's assuming this entire load of garbage isn't thrown out before then," Pimentel uttered warningly. "Anything can happen…" he added, much to his attorney's chagrin based on her facial expression.

To Landon, this was a clear threat that the crooked art dealer would do whatever was necessary to try and stack the deck in his favor—and stay out of prison. With Eddie still very much in Pimentel's crosshairs.

Chapter Nineteen

On Monday morning, Raquelle accompanied Eddie to the FBI field office for a meeting with Landon, Katie, and the US marshal for the District of South Carolina, Tony Razo.

Having braced herself for the real, but necessary, possibility that Eddie would need to relocate for a while, Raquelle could only hope that the end justified the means—and that Eddie was able to put away his nemesis.

As everyone sat around the table in a conference room, Landon took a breath and said in earnest, "The good news is that Ivan Pimentel is safely behind bars, where he belongs." He eyed Raquelle. "Bad news is that Pimentel is still out to get Eddie…thereby preventing his incriminating testimony against the art dealer and leader of a criminal organization. That means we need to protect you, Eddie, till Pimentel goes to trial…and possibly even beyond that."

Eddie leaned forward in his chair. "So, what's next?" he asked with expectancy.

Landon paused. "We'll need to put you in the federal Witness Security Program to keep you out of harm's way."

He wrinkled his nose with skepticism. "Why can't I just go back to the reservation and lie low?"

Tony Razo, whom Raquelle had been told was dating Katie, said, "I can answer that. From my experience, people like Pimentel—facing decades in federal prison—will do just about anything to avoid their fate. He's already proven that by trying to kill you more than once. Pimentel—through another hired killer—won't stop trying so long as he believes your testimony is crucial in getting a conviction. At the reservation, you'd be like a sitting duck, even if relatively safe there."

Katie offered her thoughts, stating, "Besides that, being on tribal lands would only place others living or visiting there in danger. I know you wouldn't want that."

"'Course not," Eddie concurred, sitting back.

"Didn't think so," she said equably.

"Neither of us wants anyone else to be put in jeopardy," Raquelle uttered in support.

"Then we're all in agreement," Landon said evenly.

Her brother asked, "So, how exactly does this work—and for how long?"

"You'll be relocated to somewhere in the United States that won't be easy for the bad guys to figure out," Tony answered matter-of-factly. "You'll have a new identity, new occupation, financial assistance, and a handler from the US Marshals Service to protect you—in the unlikely event that all else fails."

Landon said, "The 'how long' depends on the time it takes to go to trial and the length of the trial itself and any unforeseen circumstances..." He waited a beat. "If all goes well, this shouldn't be forever—"

But that's still possible, Raquelle told herself, as Landon had mentioned on other occasions some witnesses to organized crime activities who were never able to return to their real lives. The thought that Eddie could fall into that trap was unsettling, to say the least, including the prospect of never seeing her brother again. Then there was also what this might do to any chance of Eddie and Penelope ever getting back together to consider.

Still, Raquelle would much rather see him in WIT-SEC than on a slab in the morgue. So she was fully on board with it.

Eddie seemed to reconcile himself with it as well. "Okay, let's do it," he declared. "I want to see Ivan held accountable for stealing and forging Native American art—and giving the order to blow up my pontoon...expecting me to be on it..."

Landon nodded and told him, "We'll set things in motion."

When they had a moment afterward, Raquelle said to her ex-husband, "I know you want what's best for Eddie."

"I do," he promised. Gazing into her eyes, Landon added in a sincere voice, "More than that, I want what's best for us, Raquelle."

"So do I," she told him, just as passionate about it, while wondering what that looked like.

"WHERE EXACTLY ARE we headed?" Raquelle asked curiously the next day.

"Wouldn't you like to know?" Landon answered mysteriously with a laugh as he glanced at her in the passenger seat of his Subaru Outback while he drove down Interstate 95 South. "It's a surprise, so bear with me..."

In fact, he wanted her to do a lot more than just put up with him. He wanted her to make him the happiest man in the world—again. While giving it his best shot to make her the happiest woman on the planet, if enough time was on his side.

Raquelle laughed. "If you insist."

"I do," he said lightheartedly.

When they reached the Harbour Town Lighthouse on Lighthouse Road on Hilton Head Island in Beaufort County, Landon wondered if she had a clue about what he had in mind. If history was any indication, he suspected it might have triggered something. But he had to let this play itself out anyway—for both their sakes.

"It's been a while since I've—we've been here," Raquelle uttered with clear shock as they stood outside, gazing up at the lighthouse.

"I know." *Much too long, really*, Landon told himself, his heart already beating faster than normal. "Shall we head up the stairs?" He'd advised her to wear a pair of hiking shoes. As did he.

"Yes." She smiled at him thoughtfully.

They scaled 114 steps to reach the observation deck— both demonstrating what great shape they were in—where Landon and Raquelle had it all to themselves and enjoyed a magnificent 360-degree panoramic view of the water and harbor with its trendy shops, luxury yachts, Harbour Town Golf Links, and more.

But none of that came even close to what Landon saw as the most important attraction to him. He calmed his nerves and looked Raquelle in the eye, then said coolly, "I said that I love you. What I didn't say is that I've truly fallen *in love with you* all over again in all the ways that never really went away."

"Not even a little?" she asked cheerily but was attentive to what came next.

He gave a chuckle. "Let's just say that I was side-tracked for a minute, which I regret, while still intent on someday finding my way back to you. That day is now—and, hopefully, forevermore."

Raquelle's eyes widened. "What are you saying?"

"I'm saying that this was where I first proposed to you and you agreed to marry me." Landon removed from the pocket of his wool blazer a small box. "Now I'm asking you to marry me again, Raquelle—only this time for keeps!" He opened the box, revealing a 10K rose-gold diamond engagement ring. Removing it, he slipped the ring onto her finger, which fit perfectly, and said, "Please say yes…"

Raquelle admired her ring finger for a long moment, then regarded him with teary eyes and cooed, "Yes, I will agree to marry you for the second time, Landon—and in this magical setting! I, too, have fallen in love with you again. Or maybe the first love was merely suspended in time, waiting to be revived when we found our way back to one another." She drew a breath. "So yes, I would be truly honored to become Mrs. Landon Briscoe once more."

"Wonderful!" Landon's voice lifted an octave highlighting his happiness. He held her cheeks and gave Raquelle his very best kiss. She reciprocated in kind with her precious lips against his, setting his soul on fire with desire.

Raquelle stopped the kiss and asked jovially, "Uh, you do realize that I still have the original engagement ring—I could never let it go—and the wedding ring?"

"I figured as much," Landon told her, having kept his own ring too, for the same reason. "Same here. Those rings will always have a special place in our history, where they belong. But the new engagement ring—and subsequent wedding bands—signify a new beginning and new memories to build our love on."

Raquelle beamed. "I couldn't have said it any better myself."

For Landon, that was more than enough for him to seal the deal with another sizzling romantic lighthouse kiss.

Epilogue

A year later, Raquelle sat beside her husband, Landon, and Katie, Zach, and Penelope at the Matthew J. Perry, Jr. United States Courthouse on Richland Street in Columbia. Eddie was on the stand, testifying against a smug-faced Ivan Pimentel—who was sitting beside his lawyer, Ashley Vasquez—before US District Judge Noni H. Trujillo.

Though Landon and Assistant US Attorney John C. Potterfield—a fifty-year-old, tall, no-nonsense career lawyer who was bald-headed—felt that they had a slam-dunk case against Pimentel, they were taking nothing for granted till the verdict was in.

Neither am I, Raquelle told herself. She wanted nothing more than to put this dark chapter of their lives behind them for good. After being limited in her communication with Eddie for the past twelve months, it was generally thought that with a conviction for Pimentel Eddie was free to return to his real life. The fact that Penelope had supported him from afar throughout his being in the WITSEC and expressed interest in getting back together was a good sign.

Speaking of good signs, Raquelle marveled over her own blessings of late. Eight months of being remarried to Landon—and welcoming him back into their home— had certainly gone a long way in giving Raquelle the happiness that had been missing in her life since their divorce. Being two months pregnant with their first child was yet another feather in the blissful cap of matrimony. *I wonder if our son or daughter will one day choose to become a college professor, FBI special agent—or neither of those*, Raquelle thought, but she was more than content to allow them the joys of childhood and Landon being a doting dad first.

When the verdict came down several hours later, Ivan Pimentel was found guilty by a jury on multiple charges related to the theft and forgery of Native American art, including murder and attempted murder.

Six weeks later, Judge Trujillo—her silver hair perfectly coifed—peered at the defendant before sentencing Pimentel to spend the rest of his life in prison. Others caught up in his international criminal enterprise had already either pled guilty or been convicted on various charges related to the art criminality, with a few cases still pending but believed by Landon and Katie to be sure bets.

When word came down of the judge's impactful ruling, Raquelle breathed a sigh of relief as she and her husband, along with the Art Crime Team, joined Eddie and Penelope afterward for a much-needed victory celebration.

BETWEEN THE FBI Art Crime Team's assignments and other work-related business, Landon managed to squeeze in a long overdue honeymoon with his beautiful and seven-months-pregnant wife. He chose Kiawah Island, a breathtaking beach resort town on Betsy Kerrison Parkway, just southwest of Charleston, for some fun, frolic, rest, and relaxation in the sun and water.

It turned out to be the perfect spot for a getaway as— among other entertaining things such as checking out sea turtles and bottlenose dolphins—Raquelle got to see a magnificent theater production from a few of her former students, which filled her with a tremendous sense of pride. Landon could only imagine the sheer delight that would come her way when she got to see her own child or children blossom into young adulthood and then adulthood—while pursuing higher education—and going on to have their own families and the inevitable interesting directions from there to carry on life's journey.

He imagined the same might be true for Eddie and his once-again girlfriend, Penelope. Though they were taking things slowly the second time around, it appeared as if the romance was headed in the right direction now that Eddie had been officially cleared to resume the life he had temporarily left behind while awaiting the trial and conviction of art criminal Ivan Pimentel.

In the evening, Landon and Raquelle went for a romantic moonlight stroll along the beach, holding hands lovingly.

"I think I could get used to this," Raquelle cadenced. "Minus feeling like there's a giant balloon protruding from my belly, doing its best to ruin my figure."

Landon laughed. "Trust me when I say you've never looked more beautiful than you do now."

"Hmm…" She eyed him. "You really think so?"

"Absolutely." He kissed her on the cheek. "Motherhood definitely agrees with you. And having our first child out in the world will only further illustrate that.

Besides, I have no doubt that your figure will be back to where you're most comfortable with it in no time at all."

"I think you're right." She grinned, staring at his face. "I can see that fatherhood agrees with you as well, Landon. In fact, I wouldn't be surprised if I found myself fighting for your attention with one or more little ones occupying your time, precious as it is."

With a hearty chuckle, Landon responded appropriately, "I'll always have time for the single most important person in my life, Raquelle—which is you—while never sacrificing the needs of any or all offspring that comes our way."

She laughed. "Very good answer."

"I aim to please—always," he assured her smoothly and concluded this comfortable line of thought with a searing kiss before they resumed their nice stroll down the beach.

* * * * *

Get up to 4 Free Books!

We'll send you 2 free books from each series you try PLUS a free Mystery Gift.

FREE Value Over $25

Both the **Harlequin Intrigue®** and **Harlequin® Romantic Suspense** series feature compelling novels filled with heart-racing action-packed romance that will keep you on the edge of your seat.